The Baby Factory

CHRISTIAN MARK

The Baby Factory
Copyright © 2020 by Christian Mark

Published by Piscataqua Press
An imprint of RiverRun Bookstore, Inc.
32 Daniel Street
Portsmouth, NH 03801
www.riverrunbookstore.com
www.piscataquapress.com
ISBN: 978-1-950381-60-9
Printed in the United States of America

This book is dedicated to all the children,
born and unborn.

All the author's royalties will be donated to:

Saint Jude Children's Research Hospital
262 Danny Thomas Place
Memphis, TN 38105
PH: 901-595-3300

And

Shriner's Hospital For Children
2900 North Rocky Point Dr.
Tampa, FL 33607
PH:813-281-0300

Chapter 1
David Mills

The fetal heart monitor beeped with a fast-paced rhythmic sound. Judy, my wife, lay uncomfortably in the labor room bed with beads of perspiration running down her face.

The whole night had been a blur, from the first contractions to being prepped by the sleepy night shift maternity nurses. It was almost like a dream that was finally coming true. The nine months of care, anxiety, and waiting had finally come to an end. Judy had been a real trooper through the entire pregnancy, not complaining about any aggravating symptoms, and watching her diet. At times in the past few weeks I could really see she was straining to keep her composure.

The childbirth classes we attended together were fun and gave us a better understanding of all the events relating to the pregnancy and birth. It did a lot to relieve some of the tension due to an ignorance about the subject. They stressed in the classes that the husband and the wife grew closer together during the term, and should experience all stages of the pregnancy as a team.

My eyes squinted as the first rays of sun peeked over the Boston skyline. It was a miraculous sight, and one which I hadn't experienced since my days of Northeastern University dormitory living. The sun reflected all around the labor room, and revealed millions of tiny particles of dust settling around the room. The space itself looked different now than it had during the night, probably due to my semi-conscience state upon our arrival. The walls of the room were very high, done in off white paint, reflecting sunlight down on to the highly polished black and white tile floor. In the corner of the room was a bathroom, and on the opposite side of the room there was a stainless-steel table, which looked as though it should be in an operating room. Due to the lack of furniture, Judy's bed stood out like a sore thumb, located in the middle of the room.

The nurses had been in and out of the room all night long, making sure everything was alright. They were all very friendly, and seem to go out of their way to make sure we had as pleasant a stay as possible.

Judy's contractions seem to be coming closer together in the last hour or so. We had been trying different breathing methods, in order to relieve the pain, and to avoid using pain killing drugs until it was absolutely necessary.

She was blowing two short bursts of air, followed by a long exhaling breath. It all seemed so ridiculous at times, but Judy said it did the trick.

Suddenly, the door to our room opened and two nurses walked in followed by a smaller middle eastern looking woman. The two nurses were not the two I remembered during the night. One was small, with long back hair done up in a bun a top of her head, very rosy cheeks, and piercing blue eyes. The other looked older, heavy set, with dirty blond hair, and a wide pug face.

"Good morning Mr. and Mrs. Mills. How was your night?" the heavy girl said in a strong Irish brogue. "My name is Coleen McKay, and this is Susan Church. We'll be staying with you for the duration."

I reached over the edge of the bed and shook hands with both girls. "Nice to meet both of you," I said in a semi-rehearsed calm voice.

"When will Doctor Levine be here?" Judy forced out in a meek whisper.

Ms. McKay turned and grabbed the woman behind her by the arm, "Oh, he will be here in a short time. He just stopped by his office on the way in. By the way, this is Dr. Tahir Shabbir, the resident obstetrician. She is going to check you over now, to make sure everything is in order."

The doctor took the hospital chart from the end of the bed and began flipping through the chart. Her expression never changed. Most of her communication was done through a series of nods and gestures. I suspected that her English was not in good order, although she had gone to medical school in the United States. Her initial check took five minutes. Afterwards she conferred with Ms. McKay and Susan Church, then gave Judy a slight smile and left without saying a word.

"Is everything alright?" I asked the nurses.

"Yes. Everything is just fine Mr. Mills," Ms. McKay said reassuringly. "Doctor Shabbir is not very personable, but knows her business. She said Judy is doing fine and should deliver in about an hour. Why don't you go down to the hospital cafeteria and grab something to eat? We will stay with Judy and keep her comfortable."

3

I looked over at Judy to see if it was all right. "I don't know," I said. "Suppose something happens while I'm downstairs?"

"Mr. Mills, nothing is going to happen for a while yet," Ms. McKay said. "You need to keep up your strength during this time."

"Well, I am pretty hungry..." I glanced over at Judy, and she forced a smile, and said "Go ahead, dear."

As I walked down to the elevator banks, it was evident that the sleepy hospital I had entered seven hours before had come back to life. The doctors , nurses, and orderlies were busy scurrying from room to room, carrying out their assigned duties.

The down light on the elevator was already lit, with a small crowd waiting to board it. The light went out and a harsh ding followed. The doors opened, and in the middle of the elevator was an old man on a gurney covered with a sheet, accompanied by a young orderly. The man on the gurney looked very nervous as the passengers crowded in. His eyes were darting around but nobody paid any attention to him except me.

The elevator clicked into position and the doors opened with an ancient clang. Everyone sidestepped the gurney and exited. I followed, trying to calm my empty stomach.

The cafeteria was located toward the back of Women's Hospital. The corridors were dimly lit and dingy looking. Why did my obstetrician work out of such an old hospital? Although like most hospitals in Boston, the central nucleus of the hospital building was old, with the newer adjoining structures branching off into all directions.

I stepped out of the elevator into the corridor traffic, which all seemed to be heading towards the cafeteria. Once inside, I grabbed a plastic tray and ventured down the line, looking over the breakfast items. I settled for a large orange juice and a jelly doughnut, to cut down on my eating time.

As I pulled up a chair at an empty table I noticed all the different groups of people sitting around the cafeteria. Most of the doctors were broken down into groups. Those who had many years of service, veterans in the field, physicians on their way up the ladder, and then the residents.

Other groups consisted of nurses, technicians, orderlies, and maintenance people. Everyone seemed very energetic and full of life. Nothing like the way I felt on my way to the office on a normal morning. There were many voices loudly discussing hundreds of different topics. I sat there quietly gulping down my breakfast, trying to settle my somewhat queasy stomach.

Once back on the labor and delivery floor I made my way briskly back to the room. As I opened the door, I noticed a crowd standing around the room. At first, a nervous feeling that something was wrong washed over me. I pushed the door open further and noticed Dr. Levine standing near Judy with a smile on his face.

"Coach, you are just in time," he said in a jovial voice. "Well, take a number, and step right up to the side of the bed. Judy has been waiting for you to hold her hand and help deliver this baby."

I started to peer around wondering who all these people were. There were two more nurses on the far side of the bed with four other girls in gray uniforms.

"Mr. Mills, since your wife is the only person in labor at

this time, I asked her if she wouldn't mind letting these nice students from Boston College nursing school watch the labor and delivery room procedures. It is part of the learning process to get hands on experience," Dr. Levine said.

"No, I don't mind," I said somewhat bewildered. "Is the baby getting close doctor?"

"Yes, very close Mr. Mills. Your wife is a very brave girl. She has opted not to have the spinal medication and deliver naturally, so she will need all the coaching she can get from you."

I put my sterile smock on and began patting down Judy's forehead with a damp cloth. The breathing exercise ceased to help the pain, which was intensifying.

Dr. Levine put a sterile glove on his hand and checked how far Judy was dilated. Then he grabbed a pair of forceps, and directed them into my wife, and spun the baby into position.

Judy pushed with all her might until the doctor said to stop.

"Very good, Judy," Dr. Levine praised. "David, come over here. You can take a look at the top of the baby's head."

I sidestepped two of the nursing students and looked down. Sure enough, you could see a tiny head starting to emerge. As I looked up, all eyes in the room were on me. I blushed a little from the embarrassment.

"Well David," said the doctor, "why don't we get Judy into the delivery room to get prepared. You wash up and meet us in there. The nurses will show you where to go."

Before I could say anything more, Judy was whisked out of the labor room and gone.

Susan Church grabbed me by the hand and told me to follow

her. We entered the main hallway and took the second door on the right. It was a small room with a closet in the corner. On the opposite wall were several oxygen tanks and some other tank, which I did not recognize.

Directly to my right were a series of deep sinks and a big picture window where I could see the doctor, nurses, and students getting ready for the delivery. My hands were beginning to perspire. I stepped up to the sink and began washing my hands thoroughly to extract any potential germs.

Susan came up behind me and said, "We had better get in there, or we are going to miss the whole show."

We entered the delivery room and I was directed over to a stainless-steel stool beside Judy's head. She grabbed my hand very tightly as I sat down. "It's all right honey. We are almost there," I confided to her. She gave me a halfhearted smile.

Nurse Mckay put an oxygen mask over Judy's nose and mouth, and told her to breath slowly, which seemed to relax her somewhat.

Dr. Levine told another nurse to adjust a round mirror located on the ceiling to enable Judy and I to see the delivery. As she moved it around, the baby's head came into focus.

"Okay," I said. "We can see perfectly."

Dr. Levine's expression seemed to change from one of concentration to one of concern.

"Nurse McKay," he shouted, "get Dr. Johnson up here immediately. I think we have a problem." Dr Levine's face showed all I needed to know.

The nurse left the room without a word.

"What's the matter Dr. Levine?" I said nervously.

"The baby's breathing seems to be erratic, so I'm going to have Dr. Johnson, our staff pediatrician, check the baby over when the baby is delivered."

I looked back at Judy. She had a very concerned look through her pale complexion, and her pain was coming to a crescendo now. There was no masking the pain anymore. One big push, and the baby came out of the birth canal.

"It's a boy!" shouted Dr. Levine, trying to raise our spirits.

We really couldn't enjoy the moment entirely until the doctor gave the baby the seal of approval. Just as the doctor was snipping the umbilical cord and cleaning off the baby, a man entered the room. It was obviously Dr. Johnson. He was a tall thin man, with short dark hair and shiny blue eyes. His voice and manner were indicative of an Ivy League medical school.

Dr. Levine carried the baby immediately over to a small examination table, with two bright lights shining down on it. Some type of breathing apparatus was also being set up for the baby. The two doctors were conferring beside the table. I strained to hear what was being said. I thought I heard Dr. Johnson say something like "respiratory distress," but wasn't sure.

Dr. Levine walked over without saying a word and began removing the afterbirth from Judy. You could see the nervous tension written all over his face.

"Is the baby all right doctor?" Judy exclaimed nervously. "How is his breathing now?"

The doctor looked up while he was stitching up Judy. "I'm not exactly sure yet Judy. Let Dr. Johnson work on your baby, and you just rest with David."

While waiting for our baby to make his first sounds I looked around the delivery room and noticed most of the people who had been in the room had vanished. The resident pediatrician and the BC nursing students had left the room. All that was left were Dr. Levine, Dr. Johnson, and Nurse McKay, who were over at the table to the left working on the baby, and Nurse Church, hovering around Judy and I to keep us from freaking out.

I kept trying to reassure Judy that everything would be alright, but no matter what I said the both of us remained on edge. Judy asked Nurse Church for a phone to call her parents and bring them up to date, but there were no phones in the room, and if a phone was brought in it could have germs. The clock on the wall read eleven thirty-two A.M. The minutes ticked by like hours. Judy began to whimper softly. I took her hand to comfort her.

"Don't worry Judy, everything will be okay. I know it." Nurse Church looked at me through her mask with a very concerned look.

I bent down and gave Judy a comforting hug. Just then Dr. Johnson and nurse McKay left the room with our baby, and Dr. Levine turned looking both tired and dejected. Both Judy and I looked for a positive smile, but none was forthcoming.

"I'm sorry Mr. and Mrs Mills. The baby didn't make it. Dr. Johnson tried his best to resuscitate him, but he could not sustain any sort of consistent respirations."

Judy's eyes immediately filled up with tears, and she rolled over, looking out the window.

"But how could this happen doctor? It's the 1980s, not the

9

dark ages," I said, shocked. "Everything was going along fine!"

Dr. Levine put his hand on my shoulder trying to console me.

"The cord was curled around the baby's neck, and we did not realize it until he was almost down the birth canal. It got tighter and tighter, and we didn't see it. It is a very rare instance, and there are no symptoms during the final stages of pregnancy. It is so rare that most expecting couples are not made aware of this possibility. I know it's a shock, but please don't let this stop you from trying to have a family."

I just stood there, looking past Dr. Levine, trying to imagine the immediate future for Judy and I, and explain to her parents and mine what just happened. I knew that in any pregnancy there were risks, but the unfairness of it all unnerved me. Over the intercom system a young woman was calling a code to Cardiology. My mind just drifted.

Chapter 2
David Mills

Judy plunged a wooden ladle down into the pot of spaghetti sauce and brought a small portion to her lips. She cooled it with her breath, and then took a taste. It had been a long time since she made spaghetti and meatballs, but it was Kevin Allen's favorite.

I had been working out in the garden all day, and decided to come in and freshen up and see if Judy needed any last-minute chores done. From the dining room I could see her cooking away. Judy was a good cook, and even though I would have married her anyway, it was a great fringe benefit. So many guys my age used to tell me how they suffered along for a couple of years on bad cooking until their wives got the hang of preparing a good meal.

It had been almost a month now since our baby's death, and Judy was still depressed most of the time. I gave her as much comfort as I could, but she would have to work most of it out herself, and with her therapist. A nurse at Women's Hospital also had a therapy group that met once a week in Boston. This was specific to women who had gone through the same traumatic experience.

The whole process of birth, which was supposed to be such a special time for us, had turned out to be a shattering experience filled with disappointment. Judy had carried a living being for nine months, never abusing herself, and always eating right and getting the proper sleep. The stretch marks on her stomach were proof that she had been pregnant, but somehow had nothing to show for it.

I think the hardest thing for both of us was to dismantle the baby's room. As much as I tried to put the episode behind us, I knew it would always be there. I insisted on putting the baby's things away, taking the room apart, and making an office or a sitting room out of it. She was told by the visiting nurse that it was better for her psychologically if we both did it together. Judy always said it was bad luck to buy or receive gifts and set up the room before the baby was born, but it was more practical. Never having been an expectant father, I told her it was ridiculous not to prepare for a baby both mentally and financially. The price of baby furniture and accessories was astronomical.

The whole experience was so disheartening and frightening, that I wondered if this would spoil our chances for another child in the future.

As I gazed out the living room window, I saw a red sports car pull up into our driveway. My friend Kevin Allen emerged from the car taking off his sunglasses and dropping them onto the seat of the car. He brushed his dirty blonde hair from his eyes as he walked up the brick path to our front door. His clothes as always were expensive and stylish, contrasting my usual conservative dress.

Kevin had been one of my closest friends growing up. Since grammar school we had been together, and grew to be more like brothers than friends. We graduated from the same high school some fifteen years ago, and even double dated with our girlfriends to the senior prom. He was a ladies man, and set me up with a great date to the prom. We were a couple of wandering spirits during high school, and wanted something different upon graduation. Kevin and I decided to join the army, to the dismay of my parents and his. The war in Vietnam was raging at that time, and most people were drafted if they did not enlist.

To our parent's dismay, we decided to enlist so we could get the job we wanted and were rushed through six weeks of boot camp. Before we knew it, our plane was touching down in Cam Rau Bay, South Vietnam. We were assigned to an engineering unit stationed in the central highlands. Somehow, we were caught in a crazy war that nobody wanted to win. Here we were fighting for a principle of stopping communist aggression in South East Asia and back home Washington was playing politics with American lives and American youths were conducting anti-war marches on the nation's college campuses.

One day while on foot patrol backing up a road repair crew, Kevin saved my life. I was riding with a guy named Al Secord from Alabama. He was a good old boy, and tough as nails. Kevin was right beside the jeep checking for any hidden land mines, when out of nowhere came a Vietcong hand grenade, which lodged itself under the passenger seat of the jeep. My first instinct was to get it. I began fumbling around looking for it when my uniform got caught on a rusty seat spring. I pulled my hand back violently but could not pry myself loose. Al bailed out over the side without a word.

Critical seconds ticked by with the grenade only inches from my nose. All of a sudden, a strong forearm grabbed me around the stomach, and jerked my body back with devastating power. After that, all I remember was rolling down a steep grassy hill with machine gun fire echoing in the air.

When I finally stopped rolling, I looked up. A few feet away was Kevin perched on his knees, looking at me with a smirk on his face. I asked him what was so funny and he replied that I had broken my nose. We both just sat and laughed while the sergeant kept yelling at us down the hill side.

Once we returned from Vietnam, both of us cashed in on our veteran's benefits and attended Northeastern University. I majored in math and Kevin took a criminal justice curriculum. Upon graduation, I went to work for a major life insurance company in Boston, and Kevin joined the Boston Police Department as a new recruit and became a street cop. He worked his way up to detective in a very short period of time, since he had a knack of solving crimes and had picked up many investigative tricks from the street. Unfortunately, he got into the middle of a drug bust gone bad and was shot near the spine. He was partially paralyzed for a time, and still wanted to work, but the Boston Policemen's union said no way and he was given a disability pension. He then pursued a head of security job with a local computer firm in Waltham.

"How goes it old boy?" Kevin asked.

"Pretty good," I responded. "Just trying to keep this little yard from looking like a jungle. The lawnmower has been giving me fits lately."

Kevin chuckled. "Well I tell you what, I'll give you my Sears charge, and you can go buy a brand new one!"

"So how much will this cost me?" I asked with suspicion.

"Only twenty percent interest." Kevin began laughing.

"I think I'll stick with this piece of junk for a while, if you don't mind."

Kevin nodded, still chuckling.

"Well I hope you brought your appetite along, Detective. Judy has made your favorite meal, spaghetti and meatballs."

A boyish grin traveled across Kevin's face. "That sounds great to me Dave. Oh, that reminds me, I left something in the car." Kevin strutted over to the passenger side of the car and retrieved a brown bag. He walked back and handed it to me.

"What's this?" As I curled over the top of the bag, I noticed it was a six pack of my favorite beer. Kevin put his arm around my shoulder.

"Well, what you say we go in and see Judy, and polish off a few of these beers?"

Judy, Kevin, and I sat around a beautifully decorated table, devouring the spaghetti and meatballs. Looking down, I noticed a few specks of sauce decorating my shirt.

Kevin was desperately trying to engage Judy in conversation. He was so fond of her, and felt terrible about the baby. "Judy," he said, in a jovial voice. "This is the best spaghetti dinner I've had in a long time. It's like living back in the North End all over again."

Judy smiled, "I'm so glad you like it Kevin. Would you like

some more meatballs or bread?"

Kevin sat back in his chair rubbing his stomach, exhaled, and said, "Not for me. I'm stuffed, but I will have a small glass of that red wine if you don't mind."

Judy picked up the bottle and poured Kevin half a glass.

"Judy, the house looks beautiful!" Kevin complimented. "How do you keep it so nice?" Kevin looked at me for some approval.

"Well, I've had a lot of spare time on my hands since leaving work temporarily and it needed a good spring cleaning anyway." She changed the subject quickly. "How are things with your job?"

"Things are great," Kevin sprang to life. "The company treats me well, and not much is happening in the corporate world of computers." Kevin paused as if he was uncomfortable, and reached over for Judy's hand. "I know it's probably not a good time, but something is bothering me about your stillborn baby."

Judy and I looked at each other with utter astonishment. Why would Kevin bring up such a sensitive subject?

He looked back at both of us. "I went to a party last week at Bobby Jones' house down on Revere street. Well anyway I got to talking with his wife and she asked me how you were doing? I told her you were alright considering what you had been through. But anyway, she said her sister Jean had a stillborn baby about two months ago, and her Obstetrician was Dr. Levine."

"But it's just something that happens once in a while," I interrupted. "The doctor said there is no way of knowing."

"I know Dave, but over the years Jean's family had referred a lot of friends to this guy, and a lot of the girls have had cesarean sections needlessly, and a few have had stillborn babies. It sounds like this guy might need to be put out to pasture."

"That's incredible," I spouted. "I never knew anything about that, but maybe we should check into it." I sat back in my chair shocked and bewildered.

Judy cleared her throat. "But what can we do about it now?"

Kevin sat up at attention, and said, "I think you should file a malpractice suit against this Dr. Levine fellow. If he is not providing the best medical care for the money, then he should have to answer to somebody. This might not help you, but could help some other expectant mother."

"But Dr. Levine delivered my sister and I, plus her two children, and everything turned out okay," Judy insisted. "He is our family doctor. I just couldn't do anything like that, Kevin."

"Kevin, maybe we could revisit this some other time?" I hinted. "Let's go out on the patio and enjoy what's left of the day. Honey, I'll clear the table later."

"No, that's alright. I'll take care of the dishes and join you two men outside in a few minutes." Judy nonchalantly wiped a tear from her eye, turned her head quickly and headed for the kitchen. I knew he had struck a nerve.

Kevin and I strolled out through the white French doors on to a slate flagstone patio. The yard had a nice serene feeling to it this time of the day.

"She's had a pretty tough time of it since the baby died," I said.

"I know. I'm sorry I brought it up. You know the last thing I would want to do is get Judy upset. But it gets me so damn mad that things like this go on in medicine."

"I know, I agree with you. I don't want money out of this. It's just not right to me. It's over and done with."

"It's not just the money, Dave. It will make the doctor answer to someone else who can judge him more objectively than us. Besides, he has probably got malpractice insurance to cover the whole thing. All doctors carry it these days, especially obstetricians." Kevin stared at me for a second, studying my face. "Look, I have this lawyer friend. He owes me a few favors from back in my detective days. Let me present all the details to him and see what he says."

"Well, I don't know." I was apprehensive. "I'll have to talk to Judy first about it."

"Look, I'll just present the facts to him, and see what he says. I won't commit you either way, alright?"

I gazed out over the back yard trying to figure out what to say. Judy and I were still decompressing from the horrible event. "Okay, but no strings attached," I said firmly.

Kevin's face lit up like a little boy in a candy shop. "You won't be sorry Dave, I promise."

Kevin started babbling something about the Red Sox, but my mind had drifted a thousand miles away.

* * *

The workday was heating up as I tried to juggle my paperwork and my meeting schedule for the day. There never seemed to be enough hours in the day to complete everything, but that's the price I paid for increased responsibility.

I reached over to the side and scooped up my coffee cup to take a sip. Cold, as usual. I would have to microwave it when I got a break in my day. My phone rang.

"Hello," I said, "Dave Mills, can I help you?"

"Hi honey, it's me."

"Hi. How are things dear? Did the haze burn off in Lexington?"

"Yes, about an hour ago. It's getting very hot. I'm sorry to bother you, David, but I just got the strangest phone call from a man. I think it was the funeral director, Mr. Robinson."

"Well, what happened?"

"It sounded like he was drunk. I could hardly understand him. He was crying and moaning, and carrying on. He kept saying he was sorry, and he didn't mean to do it, over, and over. But I couldn't get him to tell me what he was talking about."

"Are you sure it was Mr. Robinson? I never knew him to be a drinking man," I commented. The last time I had seen him was after my son's funeral.

"No, I'm not sure, but it sounded a lot like his voice."

"Well, don't worry about it, and call me back if it happens again, okay?"

"Alright, I guess you're right. Well, have a nice rest of the day. I'll see you tonight at diner."

"Love ya." I hung up the phone and sat back in my chair, trying to think why Mr. Robinson would call and say such a weird thing. I decided to call Kevin, but he was not in. Maybe he could make some calls and make heads or tails of this thing.

Chapter 3
Kevin Allen

I swerved into the passing lane of route 128 to avoid being sideswiped by a rush hour commuter. The traffic lately seemed worse than ever. The growth of the hi-tech companies in the area was swelling the highways and secondary roads to their limits. The only thing to do was accelerate quickly and drive out of this madhouse. I reached over to turn up my favorite James Taylor song.

Things around the company headquarters had been less than exciting lately, but the regular hours were a nice change of pace. It gave me a chance to catch up on some needed paperwork, and things around the house. One of my supervisors had been out lately due to the fact that he was having trouble at home with one of his teenage sons.

It reminded me of myself when I was a young kid. Always getting into trouble, and the old man bailing me out of it. It sure must be hard bringing up a son or daughter in the city. There were so many different temptations in a city, and not always enough guidance to avoid the pitfalls.

I noticed the exit approaching and pulled across three lanes of beeping horns and onto the exit ramp, shifting down into third gear. The car took the ramp beautifully, not slipping or squealing for a moment. I accelerated quickly and put the car back into fourth gear while merging into traffic. I heard a noise and looked down; my scanner was picking up a frequency of the Lexington Police. Two police units dispatched to Robinson's Funeral Home, near the center of town. Out of sheer curiosity, and with no pressing engagements, I decided to swing by the funeral home to see what was happening.

I turned the corner and noticed two Lexington Police units, with their blue and white color scheme, parked in front of the funeral home. The blue lights were left flashing with no signs of any occupants.

I pulled up in back of the second car and walked quickly up to the front door. It was wide open, so I walked into the foyer. There were two police officers trying to calm down a young girl. She was hysterically crying and hanging on to one of the young officers for dear life.

"What's going on here officers?" I asked in a semi-official voice?

"There's been a death here, sir," the young man blurted out.

"Who are you?" the other officer asked.

"I'm Kevin Allen, a former Boston Police detective, and former Lexington resident."

Both officers seemed to snap to attention after hearing that.

"Detective Allen. I'm officer Ken Reed, sir, Joe Curtis's partner. He's told me about you."

"Yeah, he's downstairs with another officer. They are sealing off the area until our print man and photographer can be located. I think he is still on vacation."

They wouldn't need that unless it was a murder. I turned around and looked down the cellar stairs, then looked toward Ken for a knowing glance that it was okay to proceed.

"Go right downstairs, sir," he said in an official tone.

As I neared the bottom of the staircase, I could hear voices coming from the back of the cellar. The hallway was dark, but soon brightened as I approached a room where the voices were becoming clearer.

The room contained several caskets of different colors and woods. My first impressions of the area was that it must be used for an embalming room for the dead people who were waked at the home upstairs. Over in the corner was a large shallow stainless steel slab with several large jars of different fluids on the shelves above. Beside them was a variety of surgical instruments lined up in neat succession.

Joe Curtis and the other officer were standing by a casket in the back of the room. My shoes squeaked on the tile floor and got their attention immediately. They both turned around together, looking startled.

"Well, how the hell are you doing Kev?" Joe said, surprised. "How did you get wind of this so fast?"

"I picked it up on my police scanner. I thought I would check it out." I stood there looking at the other officer for some kind of introduction.

"Oh, this is Detective McDonald. Mac, this is an old buddy of mine, Kevin Allen. We went to school together in Boston."

I reached out and shook the detective's perspiring hand. He was obviously very nervous.

"I'd really like to stand here and chew the fat Kev, but it looks like we have a real mess on our hands." Joe turned to the side to give me a full view of the body. "We are not really sure what we are dealing with here."

I looked over, and saw old man Robinson resting in a casket, looking like he was taking a nap.

"Maybe it was fate that you dropped by, Kev. We are not sure if this was a natural death, a suicide, or a murder. In fact, we haven't had a murder in Lexington since Old lady Woodwirth shot her husband in bed with some blonde bombshell, six years ago."

"Well, what have we got here, anyway?"

"We have one Mr. John Robinson, caretaker of this funeral home, who is deceased. His daughter came down here about forty-five minutes ago to embalm one of the corpses, and found her father laying in this coffin."

I decided to poke around while things were still quiet. I scaled the cellar stairs and told officer Reed I needed to use the head in a hurry. As I went up the second floor staircase to the living quarters, I couldn't help but notice how much the place looked like the stereotype of a funeral home. At the top of the plush carpeted stairway was an old mahogany phone stand, and a built-in seat. One of the first ten lessons in detective school was to shade over any message pad to see if an imprint of a prior message could be discovered. Well, what the hell. It might work once in a while. I began shading the top of the paper very lightly with the side of the pencil lead. To my disbelief, a name and phone number started to appear. It read JONATHAN 205-326-8190. My mind was racing at this point.

Jonathan was probably just a friend of the family. I pulled out my handkerchief anyway, picked up the receiver, and dialed the number with the pencil. After the third ring, a pleasant-sounding woman answered.

"Metropolitan Adoption Agency, Susan speaking."

I tried to talk but my throat had gone dry. I swallowed quickly. "Hello, this is John Robinson. Could I speak to Jonathan?"

"Hold on please, I will see if he is in."

After a few minutes a soft spoken but nervous voice answered, "John, John, is that you?"

I held the receiver to my ear without saying a word. All I could hear was heavy breathing.

"John!" the man demanded, "get a hold of yourself. I told you everything will be taken care of. I promise you."

Another long pause followed. I was trying to paint a mental picture of the person at the other end of the phone line, but couldn't. Suddenly the phone clicked off as Jonathan hung up.

What was this guy referring to? For some reason, a gut instinct was telling me that someone or something was dirty. I ripped off the top sheet of paper and stuffed it into my jacket pocket.

I stood there perplexed at all the possibilities. What was this all about?

I descended the second-floor stairs, thinking that I needed a good steak and a few beers to think about this mystery.

Chapter 4
David Mills

My Ford LTD moved at a snail's pace down Storrow Drive. Rush hour had passed, but the residual Boston traffic was still left over. I had decided to bring my very used car into the city in case I met up with some crazy commuters or aggressive taxi drivers. I was usually one of those weekday warriors, coming in from the suburbs to earn a living. I was lucky enough to get into a good carpool, so I could sleep or read the paper instead of dodging four thousand pound projectiles.

I looked over at my wife in the front seat. She was listening to some music on the morning drive programs, but she was not relaxed, and her face was a little red from her high blood pressure and nerves. The past six months since our little boy's death had been excruciating, in dealing with Judy's nerves and the void that it left for both of us. Things had been so promising with the expected arrival of a first baby, and we had been in such a good place to give the new child all the opportunities he would need to succeed.

Now that was all gone. Every day was just an endless circle of going through the motions, trying to get from one day to the next. Judy was so depressed and kept to herself, doing her housework and not conversing with the neighbors, and cutting down her volunteer activities to nothing. Even our dinner conversations and weekend time was sparse and lonely. Our relationship up until this time had been fantastic, and we were best friends as well as a married couple. I was on foreign ground and was not equipped with the emotional energy to meet Judy's needs.

Hopefully today would be a new beginning. Our friend Kevin had finally convinced Judy to meet with his malpractice lawyer friend. My wife was against it at first but Kevin and I convinced her that we should have his friend look into the childbirth to see if all normal procedures were followed, and it was just a terrible chance of fate that our little baby boy died in utero. I didn't know if this legal maneuver would hurt or help Judy deal with what happened. Kevin had promised that his friend Jason Wainwright was the best there was and would get to the bottom of that ill-fated day one way or the other.

We turned off at Charles Street and headed up into City Hall Plaza across from City Hall. As we passed the entrance to Women's Hospital Judy look over to me, a tear in her eye. We had not been in this area since the death. As we ventured further up the road, I kept scanning from one side to the other, looking for a parking space. Luck was not with me, and we had to settle for an expensive, overcrowded garage. I grabbed a ticket, parked, and before you knew it, we were out on the sidewalk, dodging homeless people, tourists, and commuters late for work.

My wife clutched my arm tightly as we crossed the street

and went up the stairs to the banana shaped building. It was a combination of cement with a red brick façade and little windows up and down the space. It was a million dollar location with very small windows restricting a beautiful view of the old Scully Square. As we entered the lobby, I saw an older man dressed in a very nice gray three piece suit, engrossed in a conversation with a young woman who was talking to him in detailed legalese. He was doing his best to focus on what she was saying while casually looking at her perky breasts.

I pushed the elevator button and the steel doors opened right away, and then I pushed the button for floor number four. The car started moving upward. Judy just looked straight ahead with no expression on her face. I could not tell if she was just thinking or wishing she was home in her garden planting and smelling the flavors of spring. I had spent months talking her into meeting with this lawyer to get to the bottom of what happened in that delivery room that fateful day. Everything happened so fast, and we did not get a good explanation from Dr. Levine. I knew there was always a chance of problems with any childbirth. But having one of the best obstetricians in Boston and being at a premier Boston hospital, I would have expected the normal birth of our son. As I said to Judy, we will have Mr. Wainwright look into the facts of the delivery and see if he thinks there was malpractice involved.

The elevator doors opened with a slight squeak in the door, and we stepped off into a long hallway with what seemed like endless offices, most of them being Law firms. The building we had entered was right across the courtyard from Suffolk County Courthouse, and it was probably more convenient for the lawyers to be closer to court than further away. As we walked down the corridor, I took a piece of paper out of my pocket and looked at the suite number of the firm's location. It said 422. As soon as I looked up, we were already there. I stopped abruptly and Judy almost walked into the back of me. I turned quickly, opened the door, and stepped in.

We entered a beautiful office with all the amenities, including stained walnut walls with a chair rail and painted white sheet rock, with many beautiful paintings of Boston. To the left was a big fish tank with many exotic fish that looked like they were from the Bahamas. To the right was a waiting area, with several chairs, a couch, and a nice glass coffee table with influential periodicals of Boston and the Massachusetts region. I saw the receptionist straight ahead and walked up to her desk. She was a middle-aged woman with blonde hair, blue eyes, and very conservative dress.

"May I help you?"

"Yes," I said back with as much force as I could muster. "I am David Mills, and this is my wife Judy, and we are here to see Jason Wainwright."

"Yes. Mr. Mills, I see you on Mr. Wainwright's calendar. Take a seat, and he will be with you in just a moment."

We turned and sat in the reception area. I took my wife's coat off along with mine and hung it up on the coat tree. Judy sat there looking at the receptionist, and I picked up a magazine and started flipping the pages, pretending I was engrossed in what I was reading. A few minutes ticked off the clock in the corner, and then a man stepped out from the hallway behind the reception desk. He was an older man, maybe early sixties, with graying hair, horn rim glasses, medium build, and an impeccable dark blue suit with shiny black shoes. He looked the part.

As he approached, Judy and I both stood. He reached out his hand and shook Judy's first, with a lot of sincerity, and then turned to me and gave me a firm shake and said how nice it was to meet us. We exchanged pleasantries, and then followed him back to his office.

We entered a spacious wood-paneled room, with a big mahogany desk with several piles of white folders on it, and a big blotter in the middle with several pictures of what I assumed were family members under glass. To the right was a bookcase that went from floor to ceiling with legal books from A to Z. To the left were two leather couches with a nice wooden coffee table between them. Mr. Wainwright guided us into two chairs facing his desk and then walked around and sat down. He sat back with his hands behind his head for a moment. Then moved forward and folded his hands. Behind him was a diploma from Boston College Law School. My comfort level was raised slightly since my wife graduated from BC Nursing School, but never sat for her state boards.

"I'm glad you two gave me a call," Mr. Wainwright said with a commanding voice. "Kevin Allen has told me so much about you, I feel like we already know each other. I just wanted to say I'm so sorry about how things went with the pregnancy, and no amount of money will make things better, but at least you will have the information you will need to see if any liability exists. This also would help the next family going through this circumstance."

My wife and I looked at each other for a split second, and I turned back and stated my case and my concerns with the process.

"Mr. Wainwright, I have talked to Judy, and she is still worried that this process could take months, cost a lot of money, and still end up with no clear outcome. Dr. Levine is our family obstetrician and has delivered many babies in our extended family, and there has never been a problem. Why would we want to try and ruin his reputation because we had a bad experience with him?"

Mr. Wainwright moved back in his chair and said, "I know you have a good relationship with the doctor, but his job is too important to leave it to an aging person who might be slowing down and not paying attention to all the details that could result in a mistake being made." He sat forward in his chair. "Today is just a first meeting, and I wanted to go over the information I have developed about Dr. Levine's track record in the past few years, and the medical records from your time in the birthing room at the hospital. No decisions will be made, only a superficial exchange of information, so you will have all the facts." As he finished his opening statement, the lawyer sat back in his chair very pleased with himself.

My wife and I sat there looking at Mr. Wainwright, looking around the room, and looking at each other. My eye's fixated on Judy, and as she came into focus I could see the sorrow in her eyes. I thought to myself, was this the best decision for the both of us? Was I doing it out of ego, and looking for someone to blame for a tragic outcome that might have happened under any conditions? As I focused back to the lawyer, he pulled out a file from his bottom drawer and put it in the center of his blue blotter. It contained a stack of white papers about three inches high and had a lot of yellow highlighter marking on the first page. He distributed a pile of papers to each of us, and I realized it was a copy of the official hospital medical record. As I flipped through the stack of material, I noticed copies of a malpractice insurance company's document with a breakdown of births, birth injuries at conception, and deaths. As I looked at it, my heart began to pound. How did our lawyer get ahold of this information?

Mr. Wainwright cleared his throat to get our attention. I looked at Judy, and she was looking down and had fortunately not gotten past the first page.

"Now, Mr. and Mrs. Mills, this as you can see is a copy of the hospital record and also Dr. Levine's track record of his deliveries in the past two years. I have gone over this with our resident obstetrician who is an expert in the field and has testified in many malpractice cases, and has a great record of swaying juries in his favor. I would like to go over this information with you and see if this makes you feel more comfortable that a legal process needs to be sought."

I gave a quick glance at my wife and she had the pile of papers on her lap, and had her hands neatly folded on top. I looked back at Mr. Wainwright and gave him the go ahead to proceed.

He proceeded to methodically make his way through all the information, and key in on the highlighted portions of the hospital record and the malpractice insurance company internal records. I heard words like zygote, embryo, placenta, gestation, antepartum, effacement, crowning, umbilical cord, fetal monitoring, and an array of other medical jargon that had no meaning to me. There was also a copy of a third trimester ultrasound. The conclusion was said to be within normal limits. The lab work looked normal, and the final OB/GYN checkup was normal with a viable fetus. This office visit, and testing, was just days before we went to the hospital for the delivery.

As I gave a quick glance over to Judy I could see her interest in what the lawyer was saying. She reached up and brushed a tear from her cheek, then put her hand back by her side. I was painfully hoping that she could get through this presentation and decide one way or the other.

Then Mr. Wainwright asked us if we would like to take a break and offered water and coffee to the two of us. I looked up at the clock and an hour had already gone by. Judy motioned that she wanted to continue, and the administrative assistant brought us some refreshments and then left.

I flipped over the next page, and it was Dr. Levine's obstetrical history for the past two years. It was from an insurance company that specialized in malpractice insurance. OB doctors paid the most for this specific insurance because the downside was very expensive if you damaged a new baby or there was a loss of life at birth or shortly after.

As he continued down the page, he was throwing a lot of legal jargon at us. He was doing his best to summarize that Dr. Levine's performance had gone downhill dramatically, and there were several still born fetus's and a variety of reasons why it had happened. The reports went into painful detail, and statistical analysis, and it was obvious that the general public was unaware of any of this.

My mind flashed back to that day in the delivery room. It was such a whirlwind, but I remember that when the baby was coming down the birth canal Dr. Levine started yelling to the two obstetrical nurses that there was a problem with the umbilical cord. He said the fetal heartbeat was dropping, and they had to take the baby immediately. Before I knew what happened I saw the doctor take the baby and hand it to the two nurses. They rushed over to the incubation table and started to suck fluid out of the baby's lungs and do some heart message. The doctor joined them for several minutes, and I was looking back and forth trying to calm Judy down. She was crying, and kept asking me what was happening. Before I knew it, Dr. Levine came over, and the words came out that would change our lives forever.

The malpractice paperwork said for official internal use only. That seemed odd.

"Mr. Wainwright. How did you obtain this material, if no lawsuit has been filed or any discovery has been requested?"

"We have our ways, Mr. Mills. Our investigative team is one of the best, and has many contacts in the medical and insurance fields. If we do not go forward these documents will be shredded. Based on what I have presented, this case seems like a slam dunk." He spoke with an air of arrogance.

Judy startled me. She fought through tears, and it was all she could do to talk to the lawyer, and sound reasonable and logical. "Mr. Wainwright," she began, "this information has been very interesting, and also brought what happened into clearer focus." She exhaled and then inhaled. "I need to think about what you have told us and confer with my family before we go forward."

I looked over at Judy with a startled expression, shocked at how she was keeping it all together, and thinking about hiring this firm to represent us.

Mr. Wainwright wrapped things up in a professional manner, and knew he had done a good sell job on the two of us and would stand to make a lot of money if we moved ahead. We shook hands, put our coats on, and before you knew it we were going down the stairs of the plaza. We looked across to Boston City Hall. The breeze was blowing down Tremont Street, and Judy clutched my arm, drawing me closer for moral support. I was proud of her, and was still unsure of how we should proceed.

As we travelled down Storrow Drive, the midafternoon traffic was light. We were going west, and Judy had laid her head back, to catch a quick cat nap before we got home. I'm sure this experience had been exhausting for her. I slipped on talk radio, to catch up on the day's events, and was cruising at the speed limit. Suddenly, I saw a big black car pull up beside us, and not pass. He was staying right beside us. I looked briefly over to view the driver. It was a man about forty years old with a dark complexion, greasy black hair, and a cigarette hanging out of his mouth. He did not look my way. I increased my speed just slightly and the black car stayed right with me.

I looked over at Judy for a second and saw the Charles River across the park. There were several joggers going about their daily business, and a variety of college students from the many colleges in the Boston area. My blood pressure started to decrease with the panoramic scene, when suddenly there was a violent crash. I jolted to my right, and almost ended up in Judy's lap. She woke up, and screamed. I did my best to grab the steering wheel back, but it was too late. The car exited the road, jumped the curb, and smashed through a wrought iron fence. I managed to get my hands on the wheel and regain control of the car. People were running in all directions. When I finally thought I had things in hand a park bench was coming up fast with two people sitting with their backs to us. I slammed on the brakes and the car skidded across the grass. I pumped the brakes, and the car started to slow. I braced for impact, and then the two lovebirds scattered as if they saw a ghost. The car crushed the park bench and came to a violent stop.

My hands were glued to the steering wheel. I could hear voices and people meandering around the car. I looked over at Judy, and she was looking at me in disbelief. She had a stream of blood slowly running down the side of her face. It looked like it was coming from a small cut on her forehead. Her head must have bounced off the front passenger window from the original impact. As I was getting ready to console Judy, I heard a tap on my window, and looked back to see a Boston Policeman trying to get my attention. He had a look on his face as if I had been drinking. I knew once I saw his expression I had a lot of explaining to do.

Chapter 5
Michael Lapierre

I walked into my busy office in Newton on a beautiful fall day. The leaves were turning gold, and the sun was shining. I wheeled through the reception room, said a good morning to my staff and continued on down the hallway to my office. The adoption clinic was going to be very busy today with new couples arriving, to see if they could find the perfect child to bring into their family. The competition for healthy babies had gotten so bad that married couples would do anything, or pay anything, to have the child of their dreams. The adoption environment had started to contract substantially due to the fact that relations with Russia and China had become strained, and those countries were the main source of new children for adoption.

The Lapierre Clinic was one of the most prestigious agencies for adoption in the Boston area, due to our track record of obtaining American children, with no mental or physical issues, to be available for sale. I prided myself on bringing a needy child together with new parents who I knew had the financial resources and personalities to be loving parents and offer that child the opportunity to prosper in an unforgiving world. The price was always high, but people were willing to pay the price, especially older applicants who had tried all the conventional means and had finally run out of options.

Entering my office, I glanced at my medical degree from Harvard, and regretted that I was not officially a doctor or an obstetrician, since my medical license had been taken away many years ago for malpractice. It had been a messy affair with several lawsuits, resulting in my delivery privileges being taken away at all Boston hospitals, and eventually my practice drying up. My studies in college and medical school had been so good, and my education from my parents was the best, but for some reason I could not explain how I was not a very good practitioner or doctor in the delivery room. My malpractice record had started to accumulate, and with so many disappointed patients and their families, the medical board had to intervene. It wasn't that I didn't know all the inner workings of the process, but for some unknown reason I overlooked little things that added up to big mistakes. I dearly loved dealing with parents, and children, and the adoption service was a great way to feel like I was helping the patients I was used to dealing with.

I opened my computer to look at the schedule. I saw the Farrells' name for a morning appointment. They were a great couple from the suburbs of Boston. He was a CPA at one of the big eight firms in the city, and she was an interior designer at a boutique firm on Newbury Street in Boston. They were in their early forties, and had tried every means to have a child. They wanted a baby girl right from birth, and the wife was going to take a substantial leave of absence to raise the child if one should come available. The pain on their faces and anguish was so evident that I worked extra hard to obtain the opportunity to match a child with their wants. I had located a seventeen-year-old girl from western Massachusetts. She was a runaway with a troubled family life and had become pregnant by an older man who had promised her the world and then left her once he realized she was with a child. It was the same heart-breaking story over and over. This situation left the young girl with very few options, and if she was smart enough to seek advice from any state agencies, it would most likely end up as an abortion. To a troubled teenager, with no parental support, this seemed like the right decision versus carrying the fetus to term and having the hospital put the baby up for adoption.

Fortunately, I had been able to pick the girl up off the streets, and steer her to one of our resident homes for underage, unwed mothers. They cared for her every need, and brought the future child to term in a controlled environment with professional staff who could keep the girls well feed and off drugs, all while caring for their emotional needs.

This morning, the future adoptive family would be coming in to hear the good news that the child of their dreams was going to become available. They could have a family, and also give the child the opportunity to live a great life and succeed. They had been through the adoptive process with several other agencies and either were not happy with the child available, or the mother changed her mind coming down to the last few weeks of pregnancy. A lot of birth mothers had second thoughts when they were coming to the finish line, either by family or their own misgivings.

My phone rang.

"Hey Doctor Wonderful, how are you doin'?" the voice said with a raspy Italian accent. "We got problems, and I want to bring you up to speed."

"Who is this?"I demanded, though I already knew who it was, and it was trouble. "I told you to never call me here. This is a medical office, and we are conducting legitimate business here, and you have no reason to contact me."

"Calm down, Doctor, you can save that line for your patients and customers. We all are in the baby business together, so don't get all high and mighty with me. This is Vinny Rizzo you are talking to, and I would appreciate a little respect when you are addressing me." The threat was easily discernable in his voice.

"I'm sorry Vinny, but we need to talk when I get in my car or at home. I can't be disturbed here at the office."

"Listen, I would not bother you if it wasn't important, so I'm going to tell you something quick, and you are going to deal with it. Your little friend Dr. Levine is being investigated for a malpractice suit by one of his former patients, and they are turning over a lot of rocks. As you know, your associate does not have the best track record of delivering babies if you get my drift, and I would hate for the investigator to stumble across our little side business," Vinny blurted out in a convincing fashion.

"I can't talk about this now," I fired back. "I will call you when I get home, and we can discuss it further."

"You better call me back Doctor. I would hate for anything to happen to your doctor friend. It would be a shame if he had an accident or something!" Then the phone went dead.

Chapter 6
David Mills

Judy and I were cruising along Maple Street in Lexington on our way to see a new OB/GYN doctor. It was a beautiful day, and we were speeding by all the beautiful homes with their finely manicured yards and shrubbery. The windows of the car were down, and the wind was blowing through Judy's platinum hair. She had that look of foreboding written across her face. The past six months had been horrible with the malpractice suit, the car accident that severely injured Judy, and now we were having trouble getting pregnant.

The emergency room doctor and then her own practicing physician had explained to her that she had dramatic abdominal and reproductive damage and bleeding from the blunt trauma of the car accident in Boston months earlier. He said her reproductive system had been compromised, and he was not sure if she could get pregnant and carry a baby to term. We had been to several doctors in the recent past, but none could guarantee us a healthy baby taken to term. Today we would meet Dr. George Fulbright, who was one of the top OB/GYN doctors in Boston, and an expert on In Vitro Fertilization. He was a trailblazer in the field, and this was such a new procedure that we wanted to make sure he was the best. According to the literature and his website, his success rate was second to none. We were so lucky he had a local office in Lexington, not far from our home.

We meandered down Industrial Avenue by many cookie cutter three story office buildings in all shapes and sizes. Some in red brick with blue tinge shaded glass, and some with all glass with a space age design. I kept driving down the street looking at the building numbers. As I peered over to look, a car in front of me slammed on the brakes to avoid a scampering squirrel. I pushed my brake pedal to the floor and flung out my hand and pressed it on Judy's chest to keep her secure in her seat. It shocked her out of whatever world she was in now. She looked at me with apprehension, but realized she was safe.

"Sorry Judy," I said with empathy. "We are almost there." As I looked up, I saw building number 201. It was a nice modern building, with blue glass, and had high tech lines. There were several employees sitting at picnic tables having lunch. I pulled up the driveway and steered into a space. I ran around to Judy's door to open it. As she stepped out she gave me the thank you bob and proceeded ahead of me to the front entrance. I rushed up behind her and grabbed her hand for moral support. I knew she was not sure of this procedure, but we had had so many disappointments she was at her breaking point.

In the lobby I went by the security guard and started scanning the tenant board for a location. As I looked down from top to bottom, I saw Reproductive Center of Lexington, with a 3 next to the name. Judy and I turned and stepped in an elevator and travelled to the third floor. I took a quick glance at Judy and turned away as our eyes met. I'm sure she had a million thoughts racing through her mind as to what we were about to hear. As the doors opened, we were looking at the front entrance of the clinic. It had the name pasted in nice lettering across the top of the door, and inside the front door another stenciled name over a picture poster of several babies. My heart leaped a little just seeing the cute little children.

The receptionist looked up.

"Can I help you with something this morning?" she said cheerfully.

"Yes," Judy responded. "We have a ten fifteen appointment with Dr. George Fulbright."

There was a pregnant pause while the young woman looked at her computer screen, and then said, "You are right. Here it is. He has just gotten back from the delivery room in Boston and is catching up on his morning schedule. You can have a seat over in our waiting area, and I'm sure he will be right with you."

Judy and I settled into an expensive red leather couch, and both of us picked up our favorite magazine of the day and began flipping pages. I'm not sure about Judy, but I was scanning the articles and not really taking in what I was reading. My comprehension was disrupted with all this on my mind, and what the doctor would have to say to us today. As I turned the pages of the periodical, I began looking up at the big clock that was on the wall behind the reception area. The second hand was ticking at a methodical pace, and it seemed like time was frozen. After an eternity, I saw a nice young man of moderate build, black hair, white complexion, and wearing horned rim glasses. He had a big smile on his face as he stood before us.

"Hi Mr. and Mrs. Mills. I am so glad to meet you in person," he said with authority. "I'm so sorry to keep you waiting, but I had a consult in Boston with one on my patients, about a fertility issue. The client had been trying to conceive for some time, and now she is pregnant and nervous."

Judy and I jumped to our feet and I stuck out my hand and gave him a firm handshake, which he returned. Judy grabbed his hand after me

"That's okay doctor," I said. "We are just so happy you could fit us in to your busy schedule." Judy also responded back with a knowing look.

Dr. Fulbright turned on his heel and said, "Follow me and we will go to my office, so I can look at your file, ask some questions, and explain what we do here at the Reproductive Center." As he walked, we followed and talked back and forth with small talk. We strolled down a long corridor with offices and small patient rooms on both sides, with all the latest OB/ GYN/Fertility testing equipment in them.

Dr. Fulbright's office was spacious, with gray walls, a nice modern glass desk with several medical files spread over it, modern art on the wall, and a small living room set up in the corner of the room. The doctor went around to his side of the desk, and we settled into chairs directly across from him.

"I'm so glad you have decided to explore the option of IVF in trying to start a family Mr. and Mrs. Mills," the doctor said with confidence. "Many couples are apprehensive about taking this route due to cost, the percentage of woman who become pregnant after IVF therapy, or misgivings about clinical test information, and rumors like IVF babies having a higher percentage of Downs Syndrome. I want to reassure you this technique is perfectly safe, and we have done thousands of procedures and treatments. Our office has the highest success rate of any fertility clinic in the Boston area."

I looked over at Judy, and she was sitting there with a nervous look on her face listening very intently to all Dr. Fullbright had to say. Then she said, "Doctor, David and I have been trying to start a family for so long, we are really counting on this procedure to work out. I have been on an emotional roller coaster since the death of my child." Judy pondered her statement and then continued, "What steps will we need to do to get started with the therapy?"

"Well," the doctor answered, "we will give your husband a semen test to see if that is the issue, and then we will give you a blood test, an ultrasound to see if you have eggs before ovulation, and blue dye treatment to check on the condition of the fallopian tubes. This will take about a month, and then I can give you a full report on how to proceed, and your chances of conception." The doctor was flipping through our application and scanning the information we had given him, and looking back up at the both of us.

I looked over at the doctor and asked the cost of the procedure, knowing it would be around fifteen thousand dollars. Judy gave me a quick look that implied any cost would be okay in order to have a child. I was the practical one in the family, and knew everything had a cost.

"Don't worry about the cost yet, Mr. Mills," the doctor said. "Once we do all our testing, I can narrow down the cost more accurately. I don't want to build up your confidence just yet, until we have done our part. I'm sure you will be happy with the service we provide, and the total package."

We conversed back and forth for a while, and by the time we left the office, Judy was sold that this was the best option to start a family and live the American dream. I was apprehensive about the whole thing, but only because if it didn't work out, I was nervous how it would affect Judy's mental state. I tried to suppress the thoughts, but they kept jumping back into my mind. We said our goodbyes to the doctor, and made our next appointment with the receptionist to start the process. The decision had been made.

Chapter 7
David Mills

I came out of the parking garage and made my way down Claredon street heading toward the office. It was a beautiful sunny day with a heavy breeze. It seemed to always be windy around the big blue insurance tower. I was falling in line with many of my coworkers heading down the sidewalk to their ultimate destination. It was going to be another busy day at the office with many life insurance cases to be underwritten, and several employees were on vacation this week, which would make the office that much busier. My friend Kevin Allen had called me at home last night and brought me up to speed on the malpractice suit that had been brewing for several months. Attorney Wainwright brought in Kevin to do a more in-depth investigation since he had many Women's Hospital friends who could be of help. From what he had heard, some employees on the Obstetric floor were not happy with Dr. Levine, and found him to be more distant and detached in the past several years. We were building a malpractice case from interviews and statistical evidence through the board of medicine, and the hospital's malpractice insurance company. Through the discovery process they had to share their files, prior lawsuits, and loss statistics.

Judy had never been one hundred percent on board, but she was being pushed along by all of us, since we felt an old or outdated Obstetrician should not be able to practice if his skills had diminished for whatever reason. Dr. Levine had always been the family baby doctor, and this situation caused a rift between siblings and parents, due to his stellar reputation in the medical community, and the Boston area. This only added to my anxiety along with her family, the IVF therapy, and my job.

As I strolled down the sidewalk, the wind picked up at a pretty good clip, and was pushing me down the sidewalk. I began to pick up speed going towards a busy intersection. I looked to my right, and saw a young woman in her twenties, well dressed, and carrying a pocketbook that looked bigger than she was. She was chugging along in her high hells, and had a faint look of distress as the wind caused her to walk faster and faster. I picked my head up and looked ahead, and noticed the light had changed and the "Don't Walk Sign" was fully lit in orange. The cars were streaming across the intersection, and we were almost at the corner.

I felt a ping of fear creep into my mind because as we got closer to the corner, the wind was blowing even harder at our backs. The young woman to my right was stumbling down the sidewalk and from my observation, she was not in full control of her movements. A crowd at the corner had formed, and some people had their arms around the signs and light pole to brace themselves from being blown into oncoming traffic. I started running after the poor woman who by now was in a sheer panic and yelling for someone to grab her.

The girl smashed through a few surprised pedestrians waiting at the corner, and was headed into oncoming traffic. I lunged for her at the last second, grabbed her coat, and pulled her back with all my might. She stopped her momentum and fell backwards towards me. I caught her in my arms, and she looked up at me with shock and thanks at the same time. The other bystanders looked on to see if they could lend any assistance, but none was needed.

Once we got ourselves together I introduced myself and realized we worked on the same floor in the tower. I started talking to the young woman about our company and division as we crossed the street. We were about halfway across, when I saw a large black car pull out from the curb and start speeding towards us. I knew the guy had the red light, but he was accelerating at such a high rate of speed that I only had a split second to react. I pushed the woman ahead of me, and she tripped over the sidewalk, going down in a heap. I ran to get out of the way but the car clipped my briefcase, which jammed my leg and spun me around and I went down, and then the lights went out.

* * *

As I came to, I felt very groggy and disoriented. I was laying on my back and looking at the ceiling. I kept trying to focus my eyes, but I had mild double vision, and I had a horrendous headache. Looking around I could see a lot of high-tech hospital equipment, and some of it was hooked up to me. I could hear a lot of beeping coming out of many machines.

I turned my head to the left and saw Judy sitting in a chair, flipping through the latest fashion magazine. Once we locked eyes she jumped up, buzzed the nurse, and gave me a big smack on the cheek.

"You gave us a big scare, David," she said with a concerned tone. "The doctor said you hit your head hard when you went down on the street and are lucky to be alive."

As fast as the words got out of Judy's mouth, the floor nurse came in, and welcomed me back to the living. She also reassured me I was lucky to be alive, and said the IV drugs they were administering would make my headache feel better. She looked at my chart and asked me a lot of questions, but after several questions, I just wanted to go to sleep. The nurse agreed that sleep was the best medicine. She also said the doctor would be by to see me in the next few hours.

I was starting to feel tired, and looked back at Judy, trying to converse and get my story out. I started to remember that black car parked at the curb, and I was positive it was trying to hit me or my coworker. I pondered the thought for a moment, but my head hurt, and I was drifting off to sleep. I strained to keep my thought pattern going, but it was no use. I slipped away to la la land.

I heard noise coming from my subconscious. As I opened my eyes, I could hear the faint noise of a soap opera from the TV on the wall. As I looked to my right, I observed Judy sitting in the corner of the room talking to a man who's voice was familiar. As I started to wake up and focus, Judy caught my movements out the corner of her eye.

"David," she said in an excited voice. "How is your headache?"

The man came into full view. It was my friend Kevin Allen. "How are you doing, friend?" he belted out. "You will do anything to get out of work." He chuckled and was very pleased with himself.

I struggled to sit up in bed and adjust my pillows. Judy ran to my bedside and lent a hand. She was dressed up in her Sunday best, and looked beautiful. "My headache is better hun, but how did this homeless person get into my room?" I looked over, and a big smile came across Kevin's face.

"Well, you must be feeling better, since you are registering a ten on the crapmeter. I'm glad you are back and have decided to join the human race." Kevin moved towards the bed. "I have some good news for you, and some bad news. After your little so-called accident, I called some of my friends with the Boston PD, and you were in luck. When that guy hit you and ran the red light, a camera on top of the light got a picture of the car and the license plate. The bad news is the car was stolen from Boylston Street, and the police found it in Dorchester yesterday in an apartment building parking lot. They dusted the car for prints, but only the owner's prints were on the car. Any eyewitnesses did not get a good look at the driver since the car had smoked glass, and most people were running for their lives."

Judy cleared her throat and then said that the young girl I pushed out of the way was safe, with only bruised knees, and ego.

I started to have a flashback in my mind to that awful day. Was that guy waiting for me to cross the street, was he after the young girl I was walking with, or was he just a bad driver in a hurry? I pondered the thought for a few seconds when Kevin continued with his story.

"Listen Dave, the police have several eye witnesses who were on the other side of the intersection who observed that the car had been there for several minutes, and when he saw you and the girl, he accelerated right from the curb. Their opinion was he tried to hit you or the girl. The Boston PD has interviewed the young lady, and asked her about her social life, and any disgruntled ex-boyfriends. She said there are none. She has been married for five years and admitted to no distress in her life." Kevin pulled up a chair to my bedside and sat down, looked at Judy, and shook his head. "I don't know what to tell you man, but the only thing I can think of is when you were coming home from attorney Wainwrights office six months ago, that guy on Storrow drive forced you off the road. This could be related, or it could be nothing."

"I can't believe you think these two things might be related," I blurted out, then I rolled over on my side to face Kevin directly. "Why do you think someone might be after me Kevin.? I have no enemies, and neither does Judy."

Kevin sat in the chair with a guilty look on his face, and his mannerisms showed that he had something to say. "Well, I did not want to tell you this until Wainwright, and his private eye, were one hundred percent sure, but they have looked at Dr. Levine's records at Women's Hospital, and his malpractice insurance company. In the last three years he went from one of the best Obstetricians in Boston, to one of the worst according to the data."

I looked up at Judy, who was now at full attention as to what Kevin was saying to us. I thought back to that awful day in the operating room, when our life was changed forever with the loss of our son. Dr. Levine had been the family doctor and brought many of our family members into this world. He was a great guy and had a fabulous bedside manner. How could this information be true?

Kevin continued. "Listen, I've seen some of the preliminary findings. You know how this stuff goes. There is a lot of information that has to be evaluated, and weeded through before Wainwright builds his case, and maybe in the end it won't sound as bad as it does now." Kevin stood up and paced around the room briefly blocking the beaming sunlight streaking from the window. "I probably should have waited for Wainwright to contact you, but he knew you two were apprehensive, and your hearts were not into this lawsuit in the first place. My view is the more stones the private eye turns over, the worse things look."

I looked over and Judy was picking up the room, and not saying a word. I could tell from the look on her face that she was hurt, and not receiving the information well. I gave Kevin the high sign to put a lid on it, and then Judy came over and gave me a peck on the cheek, and asked if I wanted her to bring anything back to the hospital in the morning. I indicated the doctor might discharge me in the morning, and to bring in some casual clothes, since my other clothes had been cut off me in the emergency room. As she was walking towards the door, Kevin gave her a hardy goodbye, and she waved her hand in a halfhearted way.

"It looks like I am in the doghouse, Dave," Kevin said in a

meek voice. "I'm sorry if I upset Judy, but I wanted you to know where we were at, in case these accidents keep happening to you."

"You don't think this is related, do you? Why would a malpractice suit against a well know baby doctor cause any illegal activity like this?" My mind was spinning at this point because I could not process all the information and what Kevin was telling me was all too confusing. I lay back in my bed, stared at the TV for a moment, and then Kevin slumped into the chair and changed the subject to sports, and other more enjoyable things.

Chapter 8
David Mills

It was a beautiful Sunday afternoon in Lexington. The sun was shining, the birds were chirping, and we had just gotten home from Mass. Judy had always been a devoted Catholic, and went to church every Sunday. Since the loss of our son, she would go to church three or four times a week. I know she was praying for his soul, and that she was able to conceive a new baby to be born and bring into the family. She also got a job at the church. Judy was changing into her work clothes to do some gardening, and I was picking up around the kitchen when the phone rang.

"Hello," I said.

"Dave?" a hardy voice questioned from the other end of the phone. "How are you.? This is Joe Curtis from the Lexington Police. I hope I am not getting you at a bad time?"

"No, of course not." Joe and I went to college together, and grew up in the same town, but we were not that close. "What can I do for you?"

"Well, Dave, a few days ago, I got a call from John Robinson's daughter, Irene, from the Robinson Funeral Home. She had been organizing her father's estate and shifting the business over to her and her brother and sister, when she stumbled across some paperwork that looked troubling to her."

"What do you mean, Joe," I said, suddenly alert. "What is this all about?"

"It seems Irene Robinson found a strong box up in a room over the funeral home, where her father used to take naps when he had an afternoon and an evening wake, and did not want to go home in between. The box she stumbled across was filled with paperwork, and money unrelated to the business. I got the call, and from what I heard, the father was conducting some illegal business out of the funeral home, had several thousand dollars in cash, and was funneling the money to a shell company offshore."

"Joe, I'm not sure if I am following you. What does Mr. Robinson's business have to do with me and Judy? The only connection we have had with this funeral home is where we have had family wakes and funerals over the years."

"Better sit down Dave," Joe said with all seriousness. "When I went over the records with Irene she noted a leger entry which showed your deceased son's name, Robert, with a dollar amount next to it, which was far more than what they charged you for their services."

When I heard my deceased son's name, I became unglued. I thought I had misunderstood Joe's statement.

"It's listed with the same date as the normal charge for services rendered. She said there is no way to reconcile this transaction."

I walked with the phone and sat on a barstool that was just to my left. My mind was a whirlwind. I could not understand what Joe was telling me, and why the funeral director would have two sets of books. "So what are you saying Joe?"

"Well Dave, from the preliminary review by the Lexington police it looks like there was some illegal activity being conducted out of this funeral home. It looks a little more complicated than some information we usually deal with, so we are turning it over to the State Police. They can have their investigators look at it along with a forensic accountant. That will give us the best chance to uncover the truth, and what it means to you and Judy."

Joe and I went back and forth for another half hour on all the speculation, and what this latest development meant, but I still could not wrap my mind around the significance. I had not heard my dead son's name for so long that it took me by surprise. This chapter in our lives that we thought was closed seemed to be coming back to life, and I was nervous on how this would affect Judy. She was just getting over her depression, and we were trying to find a way to have another child that we could raise and love. I could not let my wife know about this phone call, and hopefully this information made sense to someone, and this investigation could be dropped.

The past few weeks had been a whirlwind with my accident and the phone call from Joe. I was having dreams of my son still being alive, how Judy and I would have affected his life, and that he would have thrived in a loving suburban home. Then the bad thoughts would overtake my mind, and I would dream of fighting the doctors and nurses in the operating room that fateful day. I was chasing them down, and ripping my son from their arms, and protecting him. Judy said I had been thrashing in bed the past few weeks, and yelling out something, but she said she could not make the words out. I did not let on about my phone call from Joe. I tried to suppress all that was happening. It was not a surprise that it was coming out in my subconscious.

I had gassed up the mower, and was going back and forth trying to keep my lines straight and make it look as nice as possible. The neighborhood always had an unwritten contest of who could have the nicest yard. Judy always did the flowers, and she had a green thumb. The beds went across the front of our house and wrapped around the sides. She spared no expense and time to make it look inviting. We would always throw block parties at our house in the summer to show off her expertise. Since the stillbirth, this had all come to a halt, and Judy was withdrawn and kept to herself. As I walked and listened to the low purr of the lawnmower, I saw Judy signaling me from the front steps of the house, and waving me to come in. That piqued my curiosity and I shut the engine off and made my way up the walk. As I got closer, I saw she had the phone in her hand, and she said Mrs. Mallary was on the phone and wanted to talk to me. She was an older neighbor across the street, and was living alone in her house. She was unofficially designated as the neighborhood watch and was always on guard. She loved keeping an eye on the comings and goings of things and thrived on the gossip of the day. She was a nice person, and harmless, so people around our little enclave played nice with her.

Judy put the phone in my hand. "Hi Mrs. Mallary, how are you doing on such a nice day?" I said with as much sunshine in my voice as I could muster. Sometimes my neighbor could be a little on the negative side.

"Well David, I'm sorry to bother you on your day off, but I wanted to let you know that a big black car is parked right in front of my house. There is a man sitting in the car and he has been watching you and your house since before you got home," Mrs. Mallory said with concern in her voice. "The glass is smoked so it is hard to see, but, he is writing notes, and I think he has binoculars."

"Mrs. Mallory, I really appreciate you calling me about this, and I am going to go see what this man wants. He might be casing houses in the neighborhood to break into later. Don't worry, Mrs. Mallory, I'm sure it's nothing, but just stay in your house and leave it up to me to investigate." I handed the phone back to my wife, turned, and headed across the lawn. As I marched across the lawn, I saw the black sedan parked at the curb. The street was vacant for a Sunday afternoon, which was somewhat unusual. I was closing the distance between myself and the car, but still could not see who was sitting behind the wheel. The windows were up, and the engine was running.

Just as I reached the passenger window and wrapped my knuckles on it, the car began to move forward at a slow pace. I turned to walk beside the car, and kept knocking on the window, walking faster and faster. As the car picked up speed, I started running, and yelling at the driver. As the car accelerated, I broke into a full sprint, but the car was pulling away no matter how fast I ran. It ran a stop sign at the end of the street and peeled around the corner and disappeared. I came to an abrupt halt, and bent over to catch my breath. After a few minutes I walked back to Mrs. Mallory's house and told her my disappointing news.

"Don't worry," she said to me with a comforting voice. "I was watching the car from upstairs in my house, and I got the license plate number."

I wrote down the number on a piece of paper and tried to leave. My guardian angel insisted I stay for some milk and cookies that she had just baked. How could I turn this down? We chitchatted for a half hour, and then I was back doing my yardwork. I smoothed over Mrs. Mallory's observation that the black car was spying on our house and told Judy it was all in her head. I did not want to get her upset, and I was not sure what any of this had to do with us or our recent troubles. I would pass this license plate number on to Joe at the Lexington Police, and see if it had any significance. For now, I tried to push this incident out of my head, and enjoy the day, but the damage was already done.

Chapter 9
Joseph Levine

The traffic was light on Columbus avenue for midday. I was not very familiar with this area, and kept scanning the side of the road looking for a space. It was a cloudy day in Boston, and this only added to my mood, but luck was with me. Up ahead I saw an older car pulling out of a space. I put my blinker on and pulled over and waited. The guy took his sweet time, but finally I was able to slide into the space by jockeying back and forth. As I headed toward Harry's Hamburgers, I hoped my Mercedes would be there when I returned.

It was a small storefront with very minimal signage, but from what people in the area said, it was a thriving business for over thirty years and had the best hamburgers in Boston, even with the new organic fad taking over. I entered the establishment and scanned the tables. There were a few people seated around, and the ordering counter was at the back wall. The place was in need of a paint job, and the tables were metal and Formica from the 1950s. Out of the corner of my eye I saw Vinny Rizzo sitting in the corner, reading the Boston scandal sheet and filling his face. He waved me over. I tried to play it cool, already horrified that I had to be in this part of town.

"Well Dr. Levine, I'm glad you could join me today," Vinny said with a wiseass tone. "I didn't know if you could get your blue blood ass over to this part of town. Welcome to my office." Vinny took another bite of his hamburger and stuffed a french fry in his mouth. The grease was running down his face, and he grabbed a napkin and caught it before it dripped off his chin.

"I would not be here except you said it was important. I have a lot more important things to do at the hospital like delivering babies, and looking after my patients." I settled back in my seat, trying to muster as much confidence as I could. Vinny was a bookie and a hood, but he was also a businessman and could be reasoned with.

"Listen Mr. Wonderful, I would not even think of bothering you and your busy life, but things are starting to spin out of control and I want to make sure we are all on the same page. Our little business venture might be in jeopardy, and the cops are sniffing around the hospital and funeral home. Before I get into details, would you like to order some food? I'm sure knowing you, this will be your last time on this side of town."

"No, I'm good," I responded. "Listen Vinny, this is not what I signed up for. You said you had everything covered, and no one would be the wiser, and now people are asking questions. I would rather put this little business venture on hold, and just keep running the daycare and orphanage in Palmer. That way things look legit. Dr. Lapierre is overseeing things out there, and with all the pregnant unwed mothers we are sweeping up off the streets, his adoption business is booming." I sat back and tried to give an air of confidence, but could see the rage in Vinny's eye's.

"Listen you little pissant, I will tell you when this little business venture is over." There was fire in his voice. "You owe me a lot of money, and this is the only way you are ever going to work it off. I will be the one who tells you when we take a break or call it quits."

Vinny pushed me back in my seat. I looked around to see if anyone had noticed the encounter, but it was as if we were alone in this place. Not one person looked up from their meal and the counter employees were going about their business, taking orders and answering the phone.

My mind drifted back to how the whole thing got started. Even though I was a good student in school and was never really interested in alcohol or drugs, my roommate at Harvard was a big gambler, and also was a big winner. He had some sort of system. I started betting to supplement my income. I was a middle-class kid growing up, and was too proud to bother my parents for money. They were older, and had to worry about their retirement. I was not bad at sports betting, and made enough money to keep my head above water, buy books, and have some spending money. Once I started my practice, though, student loans and business loans and bills kept piling up. My betting got larger, and all of sudden my luck ran out. I had dealt with one low level bookie over the years, but when the dollar amount reached high six figures, Vinny came into the picture. He tried to present himself as a businessman, but his city roots came through loud and clear. Vinny had my friend Dr. Lapierre on a string with the orphanage, and came up with the bright idea to keep the supply of babies coming, if there was a lull with unwed mothers. I thought he was kidding him at first, but after he sent me some pictures of people who did not pay their bets off, I knew he was serious. My Hippocratic Oath to administer good medical care went by the wayside, and all I could do was what Vinny said, and work myself out of this mess.

Vinny cleared his throat and burped. "Alright doctor. Sorry to have to read you the facts of life but we are going to tone this thing down, and wait for the dust to settle. I will keep a lid on the cops' investigation, and you and your nursing friends keep your mouths shut and lay low. I will take care of the rest."

I knew he was right, and my pulse started to race. For some reason the investigator for the malpractice attorney Jason Wainwright had all my malpractice suit records over the last five years, and had somehow gained access to medical records, and was building a case against me. My insurance company, that I'd had for decades, was getting to the end of the line with me. They had raised my malpractice insurance rates up to a very unaffordable figure. I could feel the walls closing in on me. I would call Lapierre and get together for dinner tonight, and try and keep him from panicking.

I walked out the door on to the street. I dodged a couple of drunks who were camped out and made my way down the street. The only thing I could hear was the purr of city traffic and the sound of police and fire engines. I walked swiftly towards my car, hoping it was still there. The homeless people started to tag along, sizing me up as someone who could spare a dollar. I closed the distance to my car and jumped in. Two pathetic faces were peering in my passenger window. I turned up the radio and pulled out, pretending they did not exist.

Chapter 10
David Mills

I sat in the seat beside the examination table. Judy sat upright in a surgical gown with her legs hanging over the end. She had her hair in a blue cap and was nervously waiting for Dr. Fulbright to come in with his nurse. At the prior appointment we had been told that Judy's Fallopian tubes had been damaged in the car accident and that is why she was having trouble conceiving a child. IVF would give her a better chance. The previous months had been a whirlwind of hormone injections, blood tests, ultrasounds, and a lot of other things I really didn't understand. All I knew was that Judy had been so emotional the past few months with all the activity. The different steps it took to progress left me wondering if we would ever get to the final disposition.

The egg retrieval had been done at the previous appointment, under conscious sedation. It was then mixed with my semen and today we would find out how many eggs fertilized into embryos. Judy and I hoped for many Grade A eggs since they had the best chance to grow into a living being. As I looked around the room at all the medical equipment, I started to become nervous. I tried to keep a brave face on, but I kept turning my head around to not make eye contact with Judy.

All of a sudden Dr. Fulbright and his nurse entered the room. He was carrying a petri dish, and rested it on a surgical table near the bed. "Good morning folks," he said with a jovial voice. "How are my two patients this morning?"

I looked at Judy, and she looked back at me, and we both gave a very strained "Good," back to them both.

"Well, I have some good news this morning," the doctor responded. "The embryos are mostly grade A and grade B which give us a higher percentage that we might have success. I know we talked about it, but how many embryos would you like transferred into the cervix?" The doctor looked back at us waiting for a response.

Judy looked at me, and then back at the doctor, and said she wanted two transferred that were grade A. She was very serious and without emotion as we talked. I could see a bead of sweat forming on her forehead. Her complexion looked milky white, and it melded in with her light blue gown. A monitor was on the wall to see what was happening. Dr. Fulbright went over to the corner of the room and started washing his hands very thoroughly, and waiting for them to air dry.

The nurse got Judy in position, laying her back on the surgical table and putting her legs in the stirrups. She then started the valium IV drip. Judy lay looking straight up at the ceiling, and I focused my eyes on the TV screen, and did not look any other way. My mind was racing with a million thoughts, and dreams, and the roller coaster ride of the past few months was just beginning to set in.

The doctor stepped back from the sink, slipped on his surgical gloves, and started transferring the fertilized eggs into Judy's cervix. It took several minutes for the procedure to take place. As I looked up at the screen, I saw a black dot moving from the cervix to what I thought was the uterus. It resembled a shooting star. I heard a sound of delight. As I looked over, my wife had a smile from ear to ear knowing the procedure was going well, and the chance of success was high. She squeezed my hand even though she was relaxed. We both looked back at the screen and followed the progress. Had a living being been born to us that moment? Only time would tell.

* * *

After the procedure was over, we met Dr. Fulbright in his office. Judy looked tired, but also had a look of excitement on her face. I tried to stay upbeat, and the look on Judy's face made me feel better.

The doctor was fumbling with some paperwork in his bottom drawer, and then pulled his head up, and looked at a few reports.

"Well you two, that procedure went very well. The next steps will be a blood test in ten days to see if the HCG is rising, and if so, we might have a couple who are expecting a baby." The doctor sat back in his leather chair and put his hands behind his head, very pleased with himself.

Judy and I jumped up from our seats and hugged, then shook hands with the doctor and thanked him profusely. As we made our way out to the car in the parking lot, we told each other Dr. Fulbright was a miracle worker. Only time would tell.

Chapter 11
David Mills

I sat at my desk gazing out the window across the Boston skyline, back towards the financial district and Boston Harbor. It was a sunny bright day, and my vantage point from this insurance tower was one of the best in the city. I could hear the hum of people talking in the background, and office machines purring. I was drinking my coffee and going over in my mind what I needed to accomplish that day. It was a busy time of the month in the life insurance business, and I knew many agents would be calling to try and push their insurance applications through in order to get paid. I had not been working a lot of overtime since I felt I needed to be home with Judy at night, and make sure she was okay. Things had been rocky for her, and I was doing my best to support her needs.

As I pondered the next thought, I heard the phone ring. I swiveled my chair around and picked up the phone from its receiver. "Underwriting, David Mills speaking," I spouted out with as much authority as possible. I heard a brief pause and then heavy breathing.

"I'm sorry to bother you Mr. Mills," the person spoke in a

meek voice. "My name is Bruce Durgan from Commonwealth Causualty insurance company. We are the insurance company who handles Dr. Levine's malpractice insurance."

I sat in my chair looking out across the office. I could see one of my coworkers giving me the high sign that he wanted to go to the café with me to pick up more coffee, and I'm sure catch up on sports and the latest office gossip. I gave him the sign that I would be with him in a minute. All I could think of was why is this guy calling me? I was suing one of his customers, and he should be working to minimize the financial damage that Dr. Levine had caused with his negligence. I sat there in disbelief for a few seconds, and then spoke.

"Well Mr. Durgan, this is highly unusual, and I don't know if I should be talking to you without Mr. Wainwright on the phone call."

"I know, I know Mr. Mills. I know this is highly unethical, and I would usually never think of calling you. But I have stumbled on to some information that if known by the public could really open up a multimillion dollar pandora's box of lying, deceit, and gross malpractice." There was a slight pause and some heavy breathing, and then Mr. Durgan continued. "My job as a malpractice claims examiner is to look objectively at claim and loss data, and set rates for the different doctors that are insured under our program. For the last couple of years I have noticed a dramatic increase in Dr. Levine's claims ratio, and have brought this to my superiors saying it is outside the norm, even for a bad baby doctor."

I sat there with the phone glued to my ear as the story unfolded. The first thing that entered my mind was a multimillion-dollar judgement, and then that was pushed out by my alarm bell going off, wondering what was this person trying to tell me.

"Mr. Durgan, I have an underwriting background and understand what you are telling me in general, but if you were so concerned about his loss ratio in regard to his profession why wouldn't your superiors contact the hospital, and talk to his immediate boss?"

"That would make sense," the man said with a sense of concern in his voice. "When I talked to my manager, and then his director they both said the same thing. They said just to raise the insurance premium we were charging him, and let his bosses at the hospital deal with him if he was not doing his job properly."

I sat glued to my seat taking in all this man was saying, not really understanding what he was getting at. "I have heard a lot of valid points as to Dr. Levine's loss ratio and questioning his ability, but he did come with high recommendations in the past, and my family and my wife's family used him for a generation. What is the bottom line Mr. Durgan?"

"Well…" There was a pregnant pause. "Based on what I am seeing in the statistics, and the way a lot of the claim reports are reading, the good doctor is either having a nervous breakdown or has a brain tumor effecting his abilities. The loss ratio is three times the normal rate, and is showing no signs of getting better."

As I listened to his story, I was getting a flutter in my stomach and I could feel my pulse starting to race. The lawsuit I had filed was being negotiated with my lawyer Mr. Wainwright, and if he would not settle, a court date was still way off in the future.

The case was taken on contingency due to the fact it looked like a slam dunk and I was a friend of Kevin Allen. I pondered what the man was saying, and thought back to that awful day in the delivery room. Was there anything more Dr. Levine could have done to save my little boy, and if so what was it? Was Dr. Levine not working with full competence? Was my son taken away because of malpractice, or was there something else going on that we could not identify at the moment. A million thoughts were racing through my head.

I wrapped up my conversation, and then headed down to the cafeteria for another cup of coffee. After my conversation I felt like a needed a drink. I was listening to my coworker drone on about the latest sports news, but my mind was a million miles away.

Chapter 12
Joseph Levine

Davio's restaurant in Boston was busy for a Tuesday night. I scanned the crowd for my friend, Dr. Lapierre, but could not see him at first glance. A young hostess, smartly dressed, with light blond hair and blue eyes walked up.

"How are you doing tonight, Dr. Levine?" She chirped with as much enthusiasm as she could muster.

I looked down at her name pin. "Well, Danielle, I am doing good. I was looking for Dr. LaPierre. I am supposed to meet him here tonight for dinner." I looked over the top of her head and kept scanning the crowd. The young lady began reviewing a reservation book, and then looked up.

"Yes Doctor. I see Dr. LaPierre's name here. I will escort you over to the table."

As we approached the table, the good doctor caught me out the corner of his eye and put down the menu. I stuck out my hand out to shake my friend's hand. "How are you doing tonight, Michael?" I asked in a halfhearted manner.

"Well, Doctor Levine, how have you been, my friend?" he shot back with a touch of anticipation and arrogance. "You are fashionably late as usual, but that's okay. You can order a drink, and then we will get settled before we get down to business."

The last comment made me feel uncomfortable, since I had thought this was going to be a casual dinner with an old friend. From the tone in Michael's voice, I knew he had more to talk about than just the weather. I sat down, flipped open the menu, and began to scan the selections. The waitress approached and I ordered a vodka and tonic with lime to settle my already frazzled nerves.

As the meal progressed and I had a couple of more drinks, I started to feel at ease, and wondered if there actually was business to discuss, or was this just the good doctor's way of establishing his male dominance. Dr. LaPierre had been my mentor during my Obstetric fellowship, and helped me get established in a good hospital in Boston. He was instrumental in giving the referrals that helped grow my practice into what it was today. I was getting lost in my thoughts, and the great steak diner, when my good friend broke the ice.

"Well Joseph, you are probably curious as to why I wanted to meet you here tonight. I know we have not gotten together in a while, but we need to discuss some serious business that has come to my attention."

I sat back in his chair and stared right through him. I looked back at my friend and mentor.

I hoped LaPierre would not say what I thought he was going to say. The last few months had been rocky with the malpractice suit, the hospital investigation, and Vincent Rizzo threatening me. The pressure was mounting. My coworkers were being interviewed about the Obstetric Unit, and my competence as a doctor. The past few months had been stressful. I was under a mountain of debt, and had to keep my business running full throttle in order to keep up with everything.

"Listen Joseph, I got a call from Vinny Rizzo a few days ago, and he is worried about you." Dr. LaPierre pushed his chair back, crossed his legs, and folded his hands together. "He seems to think you are starting to crumble under the pressure of all of the sideshow stuff that is going on at the hospital and practice, and wanted my reassurance that you were a team player, and would continue all your good work in your field." There was a pause in his conversation, and then he continued. "I would not have brought this to your attention, but after my conversation with him, you are getting me nervous also. I told Mr. Rizzo that maybe we should shut your portion of the operation down for now until the dust settles, and you work your way through your malpractice suit and the hospital investigation."

I looked back at Michael, and my stomach started to gurgle with indigestion. The words I hoped Lapierre would never say were coming out of his mouth. The one thing we had in common, besides being Obstetrical doctors, was a gambling problem. My good friend was the one who actually got me into sports betting back in the day, and it continued to this day. It started out in such a benign manner, with horse racing at the out of state casinos, and then spread to gambling on sports games and other events. We both loved to gamble, and thought we were smart enough to beat the odds, but the law of averages was against us. As the years went on and the debt got higher, Vincent Rizzo and his boys came calling, and after a while neither of us could keep up. Vinny proposed a little business venture, and even though it was designed as legit, it was far from it.

"Joe," LaPierre continued, "this thing was supposed to be temporary, and after we got back to even with Vinny, the day care and orphanage was to go all legal. You know this guy has us exactly where he wants us, and I keep telling him we need to cool it for some time until things settle. He seems to think this is no big deal, but we are playing with fire, and it's you and I who will go down if the baby business goes bad." Michael sat up straight like he was going to add something really important, and then the waitress appeared.

She cleared our dishes and refilled the water glasses, then handed us dessert menus. I tried to play it cool, but my heart and mind were racing. What had I gotten myself into? How could I continue with this foolhardy project? I tried to think about all the options that were available, but my mind was a jumbled mess. Michael waived off the waitress, looked at his menu for a moment, and then continued.

"Listen Joe, I don't care what Vinny says, we have to take a temporary break from your business, and you need to go back to what you do best. Just take care of expecting mothers and delivering healthy babies. The daycare and adoption business is booming, and I can cover some of your expenses with Vinny until things get better." He spoke with an air of authority. He placed his menu on the table and waived the waitress over and asked for the bill. My stomach started to calm down, but my heart still raced. I took a long drink of water to help settle things down.

Michael grabbed the check and we shared a little small talk.

Before I knew it, I was on the street walking back to my car. The night air was cool. I kept thinking about what my friend said, and what the outcome would be. Things had gone so smoothly for so long, I hardly ever gave it a thought that what I was doing was illegal, and unethical. The way my life had unfolded, and my gambling issues, it had been a slow ride downhill. I had hurt so many people along the way, and knew the chickens would eventually come home to roost. I needed to reassess my future and what I was doing. I had gone into Obstetrics for all the right reasons, but now I practiced bad medicine, and my world was starting to come down on all sides.

Chapter 13
David Mills

Judy and I sat in Dr. Fulbright's office having some small talk to pass the time before the doctor was going to meet with us. Judy looked a little apprehensive but was trying to keep her spirits up as this was going to be a big day in our lives. The past few months had been a whirlwind with the baby blood tests, the investigation into my accident, the funeral home coincidence, and the malpractice suit. I felt like I was getting hit from all sides. I was trying to keep things going at work and be supportive of Judy's needs, and hope for a good outcome.

The past few weeks Judy had taken several blood tests that showed her HCG readings going up which was a good sign that maybe Judy was pregnant and we might be expecting a baby. The feeling of her possibly being pregnant gave my wife so many highs and lows, it was hard to keep up with them. A few weeks ago she had some uterine bleeding, but the doctor said it was minor and the blood tests continue to rise, which was a good thing.

As I was sitting there, I looked about the office at all the diplomas, pictures, and commendations. It was an impressive collection of a life's work. My pulse was rising as the time ticked by. I started doing some controlled breathing, and then Judy grabbed my hand and looked into my eyes and tried to force a smile. I knew she must be dying inside to hear the outcome.

Suddenly, Dr. Fulbright wheeled into the office and said, "Good morning you two. How are things?" He proceeded to sit down behind his desk, and then flip open a light blue file. He studied it intently.

We both chirped in with our good mornings and small talk, but he was glued to the contents of that file. The tension was building. I decided to break the ice. "Doctor, does everything look in good order from your standpoint?"

Judy jumped in. "Dr. Fulbright, are the lab tests okay? The nurse did not say anything at my last appointment." She folded her hands on her lap with nervous anticipation.

"Well Judy, the last lab test has HCG leveling off. All the other ones were fine." The doctor studied the chart, moved his glasses down his nose, and read some of the lab values with the naked eye. I could tell looking at his body language that he was not sure about the findings. "I think everything is fine. All the other tests were going in the right direction, and I'm sure it is just an anomaly. You are seven weeks from Embryo transfer, and the only way to tell is to get you into a patient room and do an ultrasound to see if we see a little sac of life, and hear a heartbeat."

My stomach was in a knot, and I knew it was not from my breakfast or my morning cup of coffee. We had gone through so much to get to this point, and I wanted to hear the good news, not only for Judy, but for me also. She seemed to have been so lost since the death of our son, and even with time and understanding I could tell Judy would never get over it, unless another innocent life came into her world that she could nurture. I did not look back at my wife. I looked straight ahead to see what the next steps would be.

Before I could say another word, Dr. Fulbright buzzed his secretary and she strutted in and escorted Judy and me to the office nurse and ultrasound tech, who then led us to one of the patient rooms. They ushered Judy inside, leaving me to wait.

After several minutes standing in the hallway, the door opened and the nurse said I could come in. As I entered the room I saw my wife laying on an examination table, with a pulse monitor on her finger and a blood pressure cuff around her right arm. She had changed into a blue johnny. She had a look of apprehension on her face, and I could tell she was straining to keep it together. The ultrasound tech was messing around with her machine and attending to business. The nurse guided me over to the opposite side of the table and sat me down on a stainless-steel stool.

The two professionals were standing on the opposite side of the bed bantering back and forth and trying to keep the mood light. I was getting thirsty and my throat was parched due to nerves. I did not ask for a drink knowing my wife could not have a drink until all the testing was over. I looked up at Judy, and then back to the girls, and then around the room. I noticed the clock on the wall and followed the second hand around a few times, and then the office door opened.

It was Dr. Fulbright looking very serious, and the nurse and ultrasound tech jumped to attention. The doctor explained to

Judy and I that he would try and get a heartbeat for the baby, and then do an ultrasound to see what the fetal sac looked like. This would be a first real test to see if we had a viable life growing inside Judy.

The nurse handed him a special stethoscope that looked a lot bigger and more powerful than the usual ones that you would see in a doctor's office. I asked the doctor why it was so big, and I got back the obvious answer. The instrument could pick up even the slightest heartbeat from a developing fetus.

He opened a slit in Judy's johnny and stuck the stethoscope in there and started moving it around. I looked at the doctor's face as the disc of the instrument was being moved around Judy's stomach, and lower into her groin area. I could not get a good reading from his eyes; I'm sure he wanted to be a good poker player until he could confirm a new life inside. The tension was becoming unbearable, and then the doctor said, "I'm not sure if I hear a heartbeat yet. There might have been a faint pulse, but I want to do the ultrasound first, and get a view of what we see."

The ultrasound tech moved in front of the doctor and lifted Judy's johnny, exposing her stomach, and then fired up the ultrasound machine and started to apply a jell to the paddle. The ultrasound tech put her hand on the paddle to warm up the jell before she put it on Judy's stomach. All of a sudden, the TV monitor came to life, and Dr. Fulbright said to watch the screen while the test was going on.

Our eyes were glued to the screen, and the doctor stood right next to the tech telling her where to steer the paddle to get the best view of the new fetus. The doctor was stating commands like he was driving a battleship out of Pearl Harbor. The nurse and tech stood at attention, and did their jobs.

Dr. Fulbright was describing the different parts of the reproductive system as he travelled around with the scope, and as time went on, I did not see anything resembling an embryotic sac with a new life. My heart raced, along with my thoughts, waiting for something to spring to life up on the screen. I did not look at Judy for several minutes as to not add to the drama of the moment.

After about fifteen minutes, I could tell from the nurse and the ultrasound tech that the life that might have been created a few weeks ago was gone. The doctor looked serious, and as I looked at Judy out of the corner of my eye, I could see tears rolling down her cheeks. I knew her heart was breaking. We had come so far to this point, and were so optimistic about the future and our starting a family to share our good fortune in life. For some reason life was becoming very hard and complicated, and we were not in a good place to deal with it.

The ultrasound tech pulled the paddle off Judy's stomach, and started to clean the end. The nurse pulled my wife's johnny back down, and the TV monitor shut off. Dr. Fulbright told Judy to get dressed, and he would meet us back in his office in a few minutes. Judy knew what the news was going to be. The nurse and the tech said their goodbyes and left the room. We were both left there with our thoughts and prayers as to the next step in the process of having a family. My mind drifted back to little children riding their bikes and playing games in our neighborhood. How I wished God would give us a chance to experience the joy.

Chapter 14
David Mills

Kevin Allen and I were closing in on the eighteenth green at the local country club. It was a beautiful Spring day, and I could feel the warmth of the sun on my skin. The grass was green, and the fairways were manicured to perfection. As I looked up to size up my next shot, I noticed some billowy clouds pasted against a backdrop of bright blue sky.

I needed this day out on the course to blow off some steam and clear my head from all the distractions of life for the moment. Judy had been very depressed after our last in vitro appointment. She was not sure if she wanted to go through the process again, due to the amount of emotional energy that was expended to try and have a baby, and the cost was starting to add up. I felt bad for her rather than me, and I tried to be supportive. I also tried to channel her energy off into other things that would distract her from the baby anticipation. I suggested she get more involved in the town activities, church, and some new hobbies like yoga and jigsaw puzzles.

I looked off to my left and saw Kevin about twenty feet away, starting to wind up for his second shot. I could hear the crisp sound of the club pushing through the ball, and I focused on the direction of the ball careening through the air. After it was up in the air a slight wind got under it, and pushed it to the left of the green, and into a sand trap. All of a sudden, I could her some profanity in the air and my partner shoving his five wood into his bag.

I lined up my shot for a moment or two, and took my time waiting for the wind to diminish. I looked behind me, and no other parties were there. I took a deep breath and drove my club down through the ball. It lifted into the air and worked its way straight towards the green. I saw it land on the green and roll up within five feet of the cup. That gave me an air of satisfaction, as Kevin was a scratch golfer and usually got the best of me. Not today though. I was on fire.

As I put my golf club back into my bag and stepped into the golf cart, my good friend gave me a halfhearted "Good shot, Sport." I gave him a courteous "Thanks," and pushed down on the accelerator of the cart. Kevin was swilling down a bottled water and studying the score card as we approached the green. He had his glasses on the tip of his nose and was concentrating on the rows of numbers. I was thinking to myself that if he had studied this intently in college he would have graduated with honors.

As soon as we stopped Kevin jumped from the cart, grabbed a putter and a nine iron, and went off to retrieve his ball from the sand trap. I took another drink of lemonade and pulled a putter from my bag. I stood just off the green and waited for my partner to take his next shot.

After what seemed like an eternity, I could see the ball, and quite a lot of sand, come shooting out from the trap. Then I saw Kevin's head pop up to see where his ball was travelling. The ball landed and rolled up within six inches of the pin. My heart sank, as I knew he would make par, and beat me for the hundredth time. He came running up like he had won the lottery, dropped his nine iron next to the green, and strutted across towards me.

I pulled the pin, and he tapped the ball in for a four. I stood over my ball and lined up my putt. I could feel Kevin's eyes burning a hole in me, which only made me feel more uncomfortable. I kept regripping the club as my hands started to sweat. I practiced my line toward the cup, and then stepped up to the ball and took my shot. I saw the ball headed right for the cup, and then start to slow down. I had not hit it hard enough. At the last minute the ball lost speed and started to turn slightly to the left, and missed the cup by a few inches. I grimaced, and looked up to the sky to regain my composure. I then stepped to the left of the cup and tapped my ball in for a par. I knew what that meant. Kevin had beaten me by one stroke. As I turned I was face to face with him, and he had a shit eating smile across his face. He raised his hand and we shook, and then we marched off the green. He patted me on the back and his body language told me he was basking in the glory of the moment. We put our clubs in the bag and headed for the clubhouse.

At the bar, we ran into several old friends from town and chitchatted for a while before we settled into our seats at a table in the corner of the room. I knew Kevin wanted to brag about the golf game he just had, and also try to pump up my ego that

I did not play that bad. The truth of the matter was I played great, and Kevin just played okay.

"I'm so glad we could get out today, Dave. It's been way too long, and the winter did not help either. We have so much to catch up on. I can't believe I have not seen you since the Super Bowl." He settled back in his chair and looked me straight in the eye waiting for a response.

"You are right, Kevin. It's been way to long. Judy has been having some problems with the baby thing, and the lawsuit." I had not even told Kevin about what the Lexington police said about the information the funeral director's daughter had uncovered. I did not want to open up a pandora's box until I was sure it either had some importance or not. Also, I could not mention what the malpractice claims examiner had told me since that could jeopardize his job if it got out that we had talked.

"Well bring me up to date man," Kevin said with an air of command. "I haven't heard from Jason Wainwright, but I'm sure the lawsuit is progressing. I did not want to keep bugging him, since it is attorney client privilege, I guess."

I was trying to channel my thoughts on which subject to start with, the baby or the lawsuit. Both subjects were painful, and I would have rather avoided them both. I knew Kevin was interested, and only had my best interests at heart. "I haven't talked to Wainwright in a few weeks," I responded. "The last time we talked he was requesting internal medical records and setting up subpoenas for depositions for the medical staff that were in the room at the time of delivery."

"Don't worry man, just bring me up to date superficially," he chirped. "I know this stuff is probably not your favorite subject, but what do you think friends are for?" He grabbed a handful of party mix from a wooden bowl in the center of the table and popped it into his mouth.

"Well, Kevin, you know how these things go. The law moves in slow motion. I am trying to keep Judy on the outside looking in, since this is the last thing she wants to deal with. Her emotional state is fragile, and we are still trying to figure out if we are going to have another in vitro, or move on to other options." I sat back in my seat.

He sat shaking his head, and then looked up to see if he could flag a waitress to order another round of beers. "Don't worry man, things will work themselves out in time. You are getting hit from all sides, and I'm sorry I put you up to the lawsuit, but having a baby die on delivery just doesn't happen these days. I know this Levine guy is guilty of malpractice, and you should be compensated for your troubles." Kevin looked at me seriously. "After this is all over you will have a bunch of money, and then you and Judy can try in vitro until the cows come home, or maybe adopt a baby if things don't work out."

Until the words came out of his mouth I had never thought about adoption. From what I had heard and read, it was a long, arduous process, and most of the children were from China or Russia, unless you had a lot of money for an American baby. The thought kept bouncing around in my head.

I gave as much information to Kevin about both subjects as I felt comfortable with, and then we moved on to other subjects like sports and work. The Red Sox had started out the season slowly, and both of us pontificated on how the season would unfold. The only thing we could agree on was we had to beat the Yankees and win the American League East title.

After a few hours in the clubhouse bar, we made our way out to our cars and said our goodbyes. It was nice to catch up with my old friend, and I knew that the get together was worth the time. I was relaxed at the moment and looking forward to one of Judy's great home cooked meals. I pondered what we had discussed, and made my way back home in the rush hour traffic.

Chapter 15
Joseph Levine

I sat behind my walnut desk, outlining the maroon blotter with my finger. I kept scanning legal papers, and digesting what the lawsuit against me consisted of. The sun was streaking in across the documents, which made it hard to read the legal jargon in complete sentences. My pulse started to quicken as I read the charges against me and my coworkers, along with Women's Hospital. I had been sued before, and defended myself, but this was different. I had to beat back this malpractice suit, so no one would be the wiser. Attorney Wainwright was one of the best lawyers in Boston and had been in the business for many years. His track record was beyond reproach, and based on these documents, he had a very experienced private investigator who had dug up many facts and figures in this case. If by chance they could not settle this case during the deposition stage, and the case went to court, the information contained in these files could be very damaging. I knew I must go to any means to make sure that would never happen.

There was a loud rap on the door. I fumbled with the papers, pushing them back into the manila file, and closed it.

"Come in."

The door opened and Colleen McKay and Susan Church, my Obstetrical nurses who had been with me for years, entered the office. They walked around the desk and nervously sat in the chairs across from the desk. They were dressed in their blue scrubs and appeared to have just come from the delivery room.

I recalled how long I had known the women. They both grew up in South Boston and had been friends since childhood. They attended Catholic school together and were inseparable. After high school they attended nursing school together, graduated, and applied to Women's Hospital. I had met them during the course of work, and we all just hit it off. They were both very professional, and always did what I asked of them.

"How are you girls doing this morning?" I chirped with some enthusiasm, trying to brighten the mood. They both seemed extremely anxious. "The reason I invited you early this morning girls was to go over our story before the hospital lawyers get here."

"Dr. Levine," Colleen responded meekly. "We are both getting nervous, and not sure how we are going to get through this deposition. The hospital management has been putting us through our paces, worried about the hospital's reputation." Colleen settled back in her chair and crossed her legs. Susan looked over at Colleen and did the same. They seemed to feel guilty, and I knew I would have to give my best effort to have them relax and believe they were not at fault for the death of that little baby boy.

"Girls, girls, girls, don't worry. You have nothing to worry about. I have your back, and once we go over our stories, the hospital lawyers will also have your back."

This did not seem to reassure the two nurses. I thought back to the day I had caught them in the medication closet stealing pain pills. I was very disappointed in them, and as it turned out, they had a lifelong drug problem that had started as teenagers and continued on to adulthood. One of the reasons they pursued nursing as a profession was so they could steal drugs from the hospital instead of buying drugs from dealers on the street. They were functional drug addicts, and were able to carry out their duties as nurses, and take care of patients. Their childhood had followed them into adulthood, as it turned out, and I had no problem talking them into joining my little plan to make money. I would let them keep stealing drugs, and they would do anything I said. No questions asked.

I handed them a copy of the lawsuit and what each person was accused of, and as they read it, the reality of the situation became very real to them.

"Dr. Levine," Susan asked, "have you talked to everyone who was there that day to make sure the chain of command was not broken?"

"Don't worry about that. It is better if you two do not know who the players were in the room that day. Only I need to be aware of that." I flipped open the folder. "I just want to go over the details of what you are going to say. Stick to your story, and with my testimony, no one will suspect anything. The little child had the mothers cord wrapped around its neck, which cut off oxygen. We delivered the baby, and tried CPR, but the child was deceased from lack of oxygen. End of story." I settled back in my chair and looked at the two girls. They seemed horrified that I could be so callous about what had happened.

"You know how lawyers are, Dr. Levine," Colleen said. "They just keep asking you questions and talking around the facts to try and trip you up. I'm not sure we can both be consistent in our answers if they start to badger us." She kept wringing her hands, and then folding them in her lap.

"That is not what's going to happen, girls. This deposition will be in a controlled setting, and the hospital lawyers will be there to protect you at every turn. These guys and girls know their stuff, and have been through this many times. They can jump in and cut the other side off if you are getting flustered."

Susan got out of her chair and walked to the window. She peered down toward Storrow Drive, and across the Charles River to the other side. She was lost in her thoughts. I looked back at Colleen and continued on with the discussion. I was going down a laundry list of facts and a timeline of what happened, when suddenly Susan turned and blurted out, "I can't stand this!" She started to cry, and looked back out the window, and sobbed. "I never should have let you talk me into this. I would have rather lost my job and my nursing career than this."

Colleen jumped up from her chair and ran over to comfort Susan. She rubbed her shoulders and tried to talk her back to sanity. "Don't worry, hon. Everything will be alright," she soothed. "Just listen to Dr. Levine, and we will be okay."

"That's the problem!" she exploded. "We have been listening to him for too long, and if anything happens, we are all going down." She sobbed uncontrollably. "I can't even go to church anymore, and look up at God. I feel like such a disappointment."

She looked back at me looking possessed.

I was rattled by the two of them. They were starting to come unglued, and they had not even gotten to the deposition or the facts of the case. If this case ever got to court, I could not count on Colleen or Susan to keep it together. Then the whole operation could be blown. Vinny Rizzo popped into my head for a split second, and I pushed him out, walked over to the girls, and tried my best to console them.

There was another wrap on the door. It shook them out of their current state. The girls did an immediate turnaround and returned to their chairs. Susan brushed a tear away from her eye, and both of them became more composed. I sat down behind the desk, and asked "Who is it?"

The door opened, and my assistant stuck her head in and announced the legal staff from the hospital. They wanted to do a dry run before they headed up to the conference room to start the official deposition. My stomach began to churn, and I knew this was going to be a long day at Women's Hospital.

Chapter 16
Michael Lapierre

I stood in front of the daycare/home for unwed mothers, and looked over the house and the building in general. It was a gray painted shingle with a tan roof, and the yard wrapped around to the side where a small playground was filled with children running, yelling, and having fun. In the middle of the grounds were two women, talking to one another and chaperoning the kids while they were on their outside recess break.

As I looked back to the farmer's porch, I could see a couple of expectant mothers in rocking chairs talking and laughing, as if they did not have a care in the world. It always made me feel good that the women who came here to have their babies were happy and healthy. People came and people went so often that you could really never keep track if you were an outside observer.

I really didn't want to come all the way out to Palmer from Newton today. But I felt that with everything that was going on with Dr. Levine, his lawsuit, private cops, and insurance investigators, I should touch base with Sally, the house manager, and make sure everything was running smoothly, and all the adoption paperwork was in good order.

As I stepped on to the porch, the two girls sitting in the rocking chairs gave me a suspicious stare, and then turned their heads back trying to look as if they had not noticed. I continued my way through the blue wooden door, which was open, and observed several pregnant women attending to their normal daily activities. I saw a nice young woman with short blond hair and asked, "Can you tell me where Sally is?"

The young woman looked me up and down and said, "She is in her office." I thanked the woman and made my way to the back of the house and knocked on the door. As I knocked a second time, I heard a harried voice call, " Come in."

Sally was on the phone, and she gave me a look of surprise, waving me over to a chair in the corner of the room. The conversation sounded like she was talking to a distributor for house supplies and negotiating a better price for an order of baby formula and diapers. I told her to take her time with my eyes, and she settled back in her chair, continuing on with her discussion. I picked up a mothering magazine and began flipping through the pages until she hung up.

"How are you doing this morning Dr. Lapierre? How was the traffic?" Sally placed her elbows on the table and hands on her face and gave me a relaxed gaze, waiting to hear his next questions.

"I'm sorry to bother you during the week. I know the daycare is busy at this time, but some urgent matters have come to my attention, and I wanted to let you know what they are. We will have to be very diligent with our activities, and paperwork." My voice was grim to make Sally aware of the gravity of the situation. "I'm sure you have heard about the malpractice suit with Dr. Levine, and he and his staff are very upset."

Sally's eyes dilated in fright. She instantly knew where he was coming from, and did not want to broach the subject.

"Yes Doctor. I heard about Dr. Levine's troubles, but that is why we have lawyers, and malpractice insurance. Why do you think this would be a problem for us?"

Inside Sally's stomach was churning. She felt like she was going to throw up. She always blocked this part of the operation out of her mind, and pretended it was not even happening.

"I don't mean to alarm you dear, but I want to make sure all our ducks are in a row, and the adoption paperwork is in perfect order with the state, in case any investigation with Dr. Levine comes to our front door. You do know that his name is on the incorporation papers for my adoption agency, and this location. I want to make sure if any state agency comes in for an audit, or a suspicious investigator starts snooping around, that they will not find anything out of order."

"Don't worry, Dr. Lapierre. I run a very tight ship, and my girls are clean, drug free, and taken good care of. We don't coerce them in any way, and after their child is born they are free to go back home to their prior life, or we offer to give them education and or training for a job in the future. I only want what's best for my girls, and I try very hard to deliver on that promise in order to have them deliver a happy, healthy baby."

"I know, I know Sally," I said. "You run a great home here, and have made many girls and families happy. I don't want you to get the feeling that you are not doing a good job. I just want you to be extra careful, until the dust settles with my partner." I knew I had struck a nerve and felt badly, but Sally knew what I meant, as some of the operation was not totally above board. I tried to break the mood. "Why don't you take me out front and introduce me to a few of the girls Sally?"

Sally immediately sprung up from her chair, as if I had just given her a reprieve from death row. Grabbing my arm, she marched me out through the living room and out to the porch. The two girls I had seen on my way in were still there, engrossed in what seemed like a serious conversation now. When they saw me coming towards them with Sally, they both struggled to get up to shake my hand.

"You can sit down girls," I said in a disarming manner. "I told Sally I wanted to meet a few girls from the house and see how you were doing."

"This is Dr. Lapierre, girls. He runs the adoption agency in Newton, and owns this house. He is in charge of finding good parents and homes for your children. He is doing God's work on earth," Sally said with a confident tone in her voice.

The girls looked at each other and started to giggle. They both looked about sixteen, with medium build, white complexion from the pregnancy, and brunette hair. They had nice bright summer dresses on, and flip flops on their feet. One of the girls stuck out her hand and said, "Hi, I'm Trixie. I came from Lynchburg, Virginia. Ms. Sally has been taking good care of us, and I love the low humidity in New England. If I were home right now, I would be a sweaty mess."

The girls in the house helped with keeping the house clean, cooking, laundry, and volunteering on the daycare side of the house with recess or anything else the teachers needed. For the most part that arrangement worked well, and if one of the girls was disruptive or uncooperative, they were segregated from the others until they delivered the baby, since the new child was the most important commodity.

"I'm so happy that you are having a good experience at our house. Sally is one of our best employees, and will help you with any questions or problems you experience during the pregnancy." I looked back at Sally, and then back to the girls knowing their backgrounds. Most of the patients here were from broken homes, were runaways, or had addiction issues with drugs or alcohol. Whenever someone pregnant was referred to the region's drug/alcohol center in Springfield or Worcester they were courted by Sally to come to her home to finish the balance of their pregnancy, if they were willing to give up their baby at birth. Only if they signed extensive paperwork that would seal the deal. It was written in iron clad language which helped an emotional mother from changing her mind after the delivery.

Sally had been a godsend for the house. Her credentials as an Obstetrical nurse and licensed midwife were second to none. She had over twenty-five years of experience at Baystate Medical Center in Springfield, and fit the criteria of a lot of my associates. She had been a former drug addict on prescription drugs, and had been stealing them and abusing them for years at work. She seemed like a model employee, and the staff there would have never suspected a thing. Fortunately for me, an old friend at Baystate had suspected drug theft on the floor, and narrowed it down to her.

At the time, I was looking to staff the new daycare/resident home for expecting mothers, and reached out to him for someone that matched Sally's background. I then approached her at work and told her what I suspected, and that I would refer her to human resources for an internal investigation. I then offered her the position at the new home in Palmer and gave her no choice but to accept the position or leave her current position under a cloud of controversy. She made the right decision, and had fit into the operation as though she had been one of the founding members.

Sally and I chitchatted with the girls for a few more minutes, and then returned to her office to get into a more detailed discussion on what she should be looking out for. I personally looked though all the adoptions of the past six months to make sure the files were complete and in good order. Then even the most experienced State Department of Health auditor would find everything okay.

Driving down the Mass Turnpike back towards Boston, I felt better about what I had seen, and was happy I made the effort to review the operation. I started to daydream about all the families that I had helped over the years, and the looks on their faces when I had told them I had a beautiful baby that they could adopt.

I tried to keep that thought for a moment and not let any of the underhanded illegal dealings creep back into my mind. I turned up the radio and hit the accelerator, and took in all the sunshine.

Chapter 17
Judy Mills

I squinted my eyes as the sunlight fractured through the stained-glass window at Saint Joseph's Church in Lexington. I had just finished attending the eight o'clock Mass presided over by Father Joseph Burke. He had been the long-standing pastor and had married David and I in this same church several years ago. I daydreamed for a second that the two of us were standing up on the altar, and about how happy we were on that beautiful May day. My mother and father had been there, along with David's parents, family members, and several friends. We had both grown up in Lexington and gone through the school system, and both sets of parents were actively involved in the community. It seemed like it was just yesterday, but so much had happened to our lives since.

I said a few extra prayers before leaving the church area and walking over across the hall to the rectory offices, where I was an administrative assistant and all-around trouble shooter. I had Father Burke hear my confession several months ago after I had gone through IVF therapy, even though it did not produce a child. I was devastated by the news that a new life had not been created, but also knew that this was against the Catholic Church's teachings to try and create a life in this way. The priest instructed me that the only way to bring a new life into the world was for a man and woman to procreate, and that IVF was a biological and scientific means that was carried out by medical people and scientists, and not done in a natural way.

I knew this before I started the procedure with David and the IVF doctor, but I yearned for a new baby after the death of my own that fateful day, and felt it was not a sin. Father Burke was very understanding, and my penance was minor, and he was well aware of our recent troubles. He had counseled me for months after the death of Robert, and said it was God's will and he would bless us with a new child when we least expected it. It seemed like it had been so long, and I felt, due to my age, that time was running out.

Father Burke was such a good priest, and had been so supportive all my life, from when I was a little girl right up until adulthood. He was my spiritual advisor, and confidant, and offered me the administrative position after the death of the baby.

I walked through the lobby of the church into the rectory area and crossed over into the office. I sat down behind my desk and reviewed my calendar. After a brief look at the to do list I saw many of the collection envelopes would need to be logged into the parishioner's accounts, several wedding and funeral mass requests, and resume's for the religion school teachers, due to several openings that came about for the new fall season. My heart began to pick up a beat and I felt a little overwhelmed. I reflected back to what my mother would always say: "Take one thing at a time, and do it to the best of your ability, and then move on to the next. Eventually you will be done with your work."

I was busy with my duties when Father Burke strolled by in the hallway, gave me a hardy hello and his signature hand wave, and kept going down the hall. He was a very busy man, and did so many good things around the church, and the community. He had numerous church programs for every facet of church life, and reached out to other denominations to see if he could help with their issues and fundraising needs. He had great business and organizational skills, along with a knack to inspire those around him to work to the best of their abilities. The church ran like a well-oiled machine, and several other parishes and churches had Father Burke come over and offer advice about how they could get their church to run the same. He had a disarming personality, and his sermons on Sundays always kept the church congregation on the edge of their seats and drove home a point from the Gospel or the headlines of the day. He did not preach to people, but suggested people think about things, and relate them to their everyday lives.

I reached over and opened the drawer of my desk and pulled out a brochure from an adoption agency that Father Burke had given me, when I was having a bad day and was very emotional. I was against adoption, since I wanted to conceive my own child. I heard many stories of people who went through the process and either found a child who turned out to be a problem, or did not find a child to their liking after several emotional months and/or years.

The guidelines were many, and included an extensive

application that required us to share information regarding our background and lifestyle, provide relative and non-relative references, show proof of marriage or divorce, agree to home study, criminal background check, abuse and or neglect check, and pay a fee of between fifteen to forty thousand dollars, depending on the age of the child. It looked like the younger the child, the more expensive they were, or if they were Russian or Chinese versus American born. It all seemed so unpredictable, and unorthodox, and I had not even discussed it with David. He was very conservative, and we had spent so much money on IVF that I wasn't sure how to even broach the subject with him.

The nicely designed brochure featured pictures of all the happy parents with their new children, and testimonials claiming the process was seamless, and the outcome was great. I started getting excited the more I read through the brochure, and tried to imagine David and myself as one of those happy couples in the pictures. How I yearned to have a child and complete the American dream.

I kept flipping pages of the brochure until I got to the end. There was a picture of the owner of the business. It said his name was Dr. Lapierre, and gave all his professional credentials and his background, education, and years as an Obstetrical doctor. The agency had been in business for many years, and Father Burke said they had a great reputation, and also specialized in adoption of young American babies versus foreign children. He looked so nice and sincere that my heart leaped with confidence that this could be the ticket to the happiness that David and I had been longing for.

I thought to myself, was this the right plan for my family? I would go to the church after my work was done, and light a candle and pray for God's direction. Then I would go home and discuss the situation with David, and hopefully he would be excited as I was with this turn of events. We had always had a strong marriage, and even though the death of our son had put a strain on things, we loved each other so much; I knew bringing another child into our lives would be just the thing to get us on track. I knew we could offer a new addition so many opportunities, and give that baby the life that God had planned for it. Most children came from young mothers, and other couples that financially could not afford to raise a child, or another child. It made me feel good that we could achieve our life's dream and provide a good life for all concerned.

Chapter 18
David Mills

I walked up the steps of the Lexington Police station and through the glass doors. It was a beautiful summer day, and the humidity index was very high and muggy. I had taken the day off from work to help Judy around the house, and had a nice picnic lunch at Walden Pond. It was a special place that we both went to be together, and ponder the day's events, and the future. It also had special meaning since it is where I asked Judy to marry me. I remember vividly wrapping the little box and ring up in tin foil to look like a hardboiled egg. As our special day had progressed, eventually Judy got around to the hardboiled egg and almost jumped out of her skin. We were both so happy that day. Her parents had their doubt's since we were young and Judy had just graduated from college, and her parents had a lot of student loans stacked up. We all had a family meeting once we broke the good news, and said we would pay them back for a portion of the wedding, since we would both be working full time. They were good sports about it, and gave us their support.

After we returned from Walden Pond, I retrieved a phone

message from my home phone. It was Joe Curtis from the Lexington police saying he had urgent news about John Robinson's death and activities. I did not tell Judy about the message, and just said I had to go out to fill up my car with gas.

As I entered the front door of the station, I felt the cool air from the air conditioning permeate my skin. It felt so good as I stepped up to the front desk. An old crusty policeman in a wrinkled blue uniform was sitting there smoking a cigarette and reading reports. He was about fifty years old, with premature graying short hair, and was slightly overweight.

"Excuse me sir. Could you tell me where Joe Curtis is? He is expecting me."

The officer looked up over the top of his glasses and looked at me suspiciously. "What is your business with Officer Curtis?" He sat back in his chair and put his hands behind his head.

"I don't know what he wanted. He just said to come down to the station house and meet with him." I did not want everyone here knowing my business, since maybe it was all nothing.

"Okay. Follow me." The man stood up and looked much bigger than I envisioned originally when I saw him. He stepped out from behind his perch and waved me on to follow him. We meandered through a maze of desks and chairs before we got to Joe Curtis's desk. He saw me from a distance and stood up to meet the two of us as we approached.

"Hey Joe, this man says he wanted to see you," said the officer in a put off sort of tone. Then he looked back at me for a response.

I stuck out my hand and said, "Hi Joe. How have you been? Judy and I were out getting some fresh air, and I just got your message."

Once the desk officer saw that we knew each other, he turned and went about his business without saying a word.

"Thanks for coming, Dave. I'm sorry to bother you with all this, but I felt I should bring you up to date, and let you know the latest on the Robinson case." Joe sat back down and pointed to me to sit down on a chair that was to the side of his desk. "Can I get you a cup of coffee or a soft drink before we get started?"

I shook my head no, and then said, "That's okay, but thanks anyway." I sat down and looked at Joe to continue.

Joe flipped a manilla file folder open and started flipping through papers and reports. He pulled out a piece of paper that had a lot of medical jargon and lab results. I studied it intensely, knowing many of the facts and readings, due to my background in life insurance underwriting. My job was to evaluate medical information and determine mortality risk for an applicant.

Joe Curtis rubbed his forehead like he was trying to pull the information out of his brain, and then started to ramble on about the information contained in the file.

"Dave, the toxicology report you have in front of you says that old man Robinson died from an overdose of a heart medication he was taking." He looked up at me, and then back down at his reports, and kept reading his file. "I talked to Irene, his daughter, and she said he was usually very good about taking his medication and not over medicating himself."

"What are you driving at, Joe?" I asked. "Why are you so concerned about how he died? The guy was in his mid-seventies."

Joe started to doodle with the file like he had something to say, but did not want to continue. "Look Dave, we found this guy in a coffin in his basement, dead. Now we know it was an overdose, or he was murdered."

"What! What do you mean murdered?" My heart started pounding. "How come I was not told about this. The guy has been dead for a few months." I stared back at Joe, trying to communicate my displeasure.

"I'm sorry to leave you out of the loop Dave, but there is more to the story. The day we found Mr. Robinson, we interviewed his daughter and business partner, and she said he had been very upset the past few months, and they did not know why. She said he would have never committed suicide, and then she found a different set of accounting books in his personal files upstairs at the funeral home. It showed entries from a company called Metropolitan Services Inc. He had been receiving regular checks from this company and depositing them into an off shore account in the Caymans."

I sat there in my chair thinking about what Joe was saying, and studying his face. My pulse had slowed, but I felt uneasy about where this was leading.

Joe continued. "We have had many people and our detectives studying what this company does, and where it is located. We think it is a front company for some other type of business. Based on what the daughter has told us, and the fact that Mr. Robinson was careful with his heart medication, we have decided to turn over the case to the State Police homicide unit. They can turn over many more rocks than we can, and also have jurisdiction in many more areas than we have. They also

116

have the resources to expand the investigation if need be." Joe sat back in his chair and looked at the ceiling, and then down at me.

"Joe. What do you think is going on? I asked.

"I'm not sure, Dave. The detectives and I just have a bad feeling about this, and feel we need some outside help in case it is foul play. I would rather be safe, and not find out down the road we missed something," he stated forcefully.

"Okay Joe. You know your business. Do Judy and I need to do anything at this point? She is still very fragile, and I don't want to get her anymore upset than she already is."

"No, no, Dave. No problem. We will handle everything, and not bother you unless this thing turns out to be more than we think."

I gave Joe my assurances I was happy with his oversight, and told him to keep me in the loop. We said our goodbyes, and I walked back out of the station to my car. I stopped by the Shell station down the street from the police station and filled up my tank. The rush hour traffic was forming, and I meandered through many side streets to avoid the rush, thinking about all I had heard from Joe. Old man Robinson was a mainstay in Lexington and had always been a nice man, and had waked and buried many family members in my family and Judy's. He was a solid guy, and a rock of support during turbulent times for so many families in the area. I just could not get it out of my head that he would ever take his life. I did not want to even think there was foul play that had come to our sleepy little suburban town. I pondered the thought as I weaved my way home.

Chapter 19
David Mills

I heard the crack of the bat on the ball as I looked over my shoulder for the beer vendor at Fenway Park. It was a beautiful mid-summer night in Boston, and America's favorite pastime was in full swing. The Red Sox were hanging around in second place in the American League East division, but had not been playing well, due to many injuries and some of the players worrying about next year's contracts instead of the game at hand. I always wondered why someone who got paid millions of dollars and did not have a care in the world could get so fixated on something that would not happen until next year.

The Red Sox were down four to two in the last part of the seventh inning. The crowd was getting bored and paying more attention to the extracurricular activities at the park. I looked to my left and saw my friend Kevin trying to flag down any vendor who would look at him. He wanted to keep the party going, and his best shot was ordering another beer. I would have to scale it back with my beverages soon, since I was the designated driver.

As I watched the Red Sox runners run around the bases from

the previous hit, I had a better feeling that they could make a comeback. The next player up was swinging for the fences on a three and two count, and missed by a mile on a change up. He headed back to the dugout with his head down. It was two outs now, and our best hitter was coming up. He was young, big, and athletic, and could hit the ball a country mile if he connected with it. The pitcher on the other team was talking to his catcher to make sure they had the pitches lined up to squash this rally. The batter stepped into the box and was greeted with a fast ball right down the pipe for strike one. The batter was upset with himself since he knew this was the best pitch he was going to see in this series. He stepped into the box and readied his bat. The pitcher looked into the catcher, and started his wind up. It was a change up, and the big batter was way out in front of this. He banged his bat on the ground in disgust and stepped out of the box. He picked up some dirt, and rubbed it into his batting gloves, and dropped it. Then he went through his pre batting ritual and stepped back into the box. The pitcher was set, and let the ball go after a big-time wind up. The ball was curving into the plate and looked outside. The batter was frozen in place, and at the last second, the ball crossed over the back of the plate for strike three. The batter hit his bat on the ground, and spun around to walk back to the dugout. The rally had ended, and the home team did not look like they had a comeback in them tonight.

I sat back in my chair and listened to a few cat calls from the Fenway faithful, and Kevin stuck a draft beer in front of me and said, "You can drown your sorrows in this, Dave. The Red Sox stink tonight." I tended to agree with him even though I was a loyal fan and watched every game on television. Kevin had gotten the tickets through his corporate job, and always was able to get good seats. We were twenty rows behind home plate with a panoramic view of the whole park. Kevin was talking about everything that popped into his mind, from work, to home, to town gossip, to sports, and then he was at a loss for words.

The visiting team was still doing their warmups, and then he looked at me with a perplexed look on his face. Kevin was never at a loss for words. I looked back at him, and blurted out, "Are you going to tell me what's on your mind or do I have to twist your arm, Kevin." I could tell from his demeanor all night that this little night out at the ballpark was an excuse to get me away from Judy so he could talk to me about something very important. I remembered our last serious conversation about Dr. Levine and John Robinson, and I was hoping it was not a continuation of the same plot. I kept looking at Kevin until he reached down inside and started telling me what was on his mind.

"I'm sorry man. I guess I do not have much of a poker face," he said with a hint of embarrassment in his voice. "I probably could have discussed this over coffee at Friendly's in Lexington, but I figured we had not been out together at night in a while, and I know you are a big Sox fan, and maybe it would blunt the news."

As soon as Kevin's words came out of his mouth, I knew we were talking about the same subject. The last conversation had not gone well, and the news and speculation was even worse. I looked back at Kevin with a sullen look, and gave him the go ahead to continue with his update. The Red Sox game was not even registering in my mind. This terrible episode was taking its place.

"Ah, ah," Kevin continued. "I'm sorry to have to break this news to you, but I was sure you would appreciate me bringing you up to date on the malpractice case, and the Lexington Police and State Police investigation. It seems like these two things keep intersecting. The latest update from Attorney Wainwright's PI is that the depositions of the people who were in the operating room the day your son died have many inconsistencies. It seems like after your son's heartbeat was diminishing due to the cord wrapped around his neck, Dr. Levine ordered everyone out of the delivery room, and then a Dr. Johnson, the in house Pediatrician was called in on an emergency basis. Kevin paused and looked down, and then up at me, and met my eyes and continued. "That left the two nurses, Colleen McKay and Susan Church, and Dr. Levine."

I thought to myself, why is Kevin being so dramatic about this whole thing. It sounds like this would be normal protocol when an emergency takes place. I looked back at my friend to continue.

"Well, it seems there are inconsistencies in the two nurses' stories versus what Dr. Levine is saying. When Dr. Johnson arrived, he was assisting Dr. Levine, trying to resuscitate little Robert. But when you look at the medical notes it says one of the nurses was over assisting Dr. Levine, and Dr. Johnson only came in to pronounce your son deceased."

The words coming out of Kevin's mouth brought back that horrific day and pierced my heart like an arrow. How I wished

Judy and I could move on from this terrible event and continue with our lives. It seemed this heartbreak was wrapped around our necks, and we could not shake it loose.

Kevin looked back at the field to view the latest play by the opposition, and then jumped back into the conversation. "Dave, the people in that room are all coming up with different stories about what happened, and there are many inconsistencies. We still do not know how your son was removed from that room, and where he was taken to." He pondered the thought.

It seemed to me that this was not out of the ordinary when an emergency happens, and it was some time ago. People's memories fade over time, and this case had taken way too long to settle.

The malpractice company was trying to lowball Mr. Wainwright, and I was not sure why after the phone call I received from his claim's examiner. I thought this would be a slam dunk, and they would just write a check, and Judy and I could move on. Now it seemed they were lawyering up and playing hard ball. I never shared my brief phone call with the malpractice insurance person with Kevin, but based on what I knew about the insurance industry, I could not understand why they would want to bring themselves so much bad publicity.

Kevin took a long swig of his beer and let out a belch. He said, excuse me to a young girl sitting next to him, and drew a sneer from her boyfriend. "Listen Dave, I haven't told you the worst yet. It just keeps getting better. They sent a notice to Dr. Johnson, the in house Pediatrician, and it came back from his son a month later that he had passed away. It seems he was in the Cayman Islands, and drowned in a scuba diving accident."

My heart dropped as I heard the words Cayman Islands. That is where the funeral director had been funneling cash as his daughter had discovered in a second set of books from his business with a ledger entry with my son Robert's name on it. This seemed to be too much of a coincidence. My heart was starting to race, and sweat started forming on my forehead.

"Well it seems from the autopsy report that Dr. Johnson died of a heart attack while underwater that caused him to drown. The island police down there said he was a frequent visitor, and had many business dealings down there over the years. This really stinks for you since his testimony would have been crucial to your case, and could have confirmed all that Dr. Levine is telling us."

All of a sudden I heard the crack of a bat, and the guy next to me lunged and spilled my beer all over me. He had reached all the way across my body to make a stab at a foul ball that he missed by a mile. A father a few rows in back of me made the catch and immediately handed the foul ball to his son, who looked at the ball like it was a million dollars. I looked back at the man with a dirty look, and I could tell from his bloodshot eyes that he was under the weather. Kevin started chirping at him, and both men stood to confront each other. I grabbed my jacket and turned my back to the man, and gave Kevin the head bob to grab his jacket, and that we were leaving.

He started to give me a look that he wanted a piece of this guy, but thought better about it. We got our car out of the parking lot at the corner of Commonwealth Avenue and Brookline Avenue, and proceeded down the street on to Storrow Drive headed west. We probably made the right decision, since we would beat the ballgame traffic, and I had to get up early in the morning to go to work.

I noticed a big black car had been following me since I came down the ramp on to the road, and was now right up on my ass. This person was so close I could not even see his headlights. I did not say anything to my friend since I was not sure if it meant anything. I continued on at a normal rate of speed, when all of a sudden I felt a bump to the back of the car. It was so slight my passenger did not take notice. Then the car switched lanes and started to speed up beside me. I now noticed it was a black, late model Lincoln, with three passengers in it. They all looked to be in their late twenties or early thirties, and looked like they were punks from the city.

As the car came up beside me, the front passenger was waving, and instructing me to roll down the window. He kept waving and giving me hand motions to get my attention. I knew this felt like trouble, but I did it anyway knowing I had Kevin with me for back up. I pushed the power button, and as the window went down, I could hear the young bucks start yelling. They were saying, "Get the fuck out of our city, and go back to the suburbs!" They kept saying with more venom every time, and eventually got Kevin's attention. I kept driving and trying to ignore them, while I made my way towards Harvard University.

Kevin reached over and turned down the radio, and then leaned forward and told the three guys, they were a bunch of pussies, and to fuck off. They started laughing, and talking more smack to us to keep the party going. The front seat passenger of the car took a drag on his cigarette, and then flicked it at me.

I pulled my head back and it flew by, and Kevin did the same. The cigarette went out Kevin's window on the other side. Kevin sat forward again and started to taunt the city kids some more. I was hoping this whole episode was going to stop, and I could get back to driving home.

I reached down and put up my window to drown out the curses that were coming my way, and Kevin was giving them all the finger. All of a sudden the big back Lincoln started coming into my lane, and was just a few inches from my door. I instinctively jerked the wheel to the right and hit the curbing. The hubcaps on that side scraped and gave a loud metal sound, and then flew off. Kevin flipped out and started screaming across me towards them, even though my window was up and the punks couldn't hear a word of what he was saying.

I had a flashback to that terrible day when Judy and I had been forced off this same road, just a few miles back. My heart was racing while I was trying to straighten out the wheel to avoid driving off the road into the Charles River.

Then I heard the car next to me lock up his breaks, and all of a sudden he fell back, switched lanes, and drove off an exit ramp to my right. Kevin yelled at me to follow them, but I flew right by the exit, and there was no way I could stop or back up. As I went under the bridge and came up the other side, Kevin said he could see the guys run the red light, go over the bridge that crossed the river, and disappear into Cambridge proper.

As I looked back at Kevin, he was fumbling through my glove box for something. After a few moments he pulled out a napkin and started writing down something. I asked what he was doing.

"I got their license plate number." I was confused by how fast everything had happened, and that he had the composure to get that plate number. I looked over at him with a dumbfounded expression, and he responded, "What. This is part of my police training. Why the look?"

We both started laughing, and I turned the radio back up, and finished listening to the Red Sox game. I knew my hubcaps were gone. Kevin played down the whole thing and tried to lighten the mood. My anxiety was at an all-time high, since I was not used to being exposed to this city stuff.

Kevin called me the next day at work, and said he had Boston Police run the license plate of the Lincoln. It was registered to a Patrick Duggan from Charlestown. According to BPD, this guy was thirty-two years old and had a record for drugs, car theft, breaking and entering, and minor assault. He had done a few short stretches at the Billerica House of Correction and was out currently on parole. According to his thick file, he was a foot soldier for one Vinny Rizzo, who was the head of a street gang that ran the rackets, prostitution, drugs, and other assorted activities around the city. Kevin continued that this guy Vinny was bad news, and had always insulated himself from all these activities. He had his henchmen do all the dirty work, so he avoided prosecution when anything blew up.

After I heard his rap sheet my mind started racing, and I wondered if all these close calls were related. Why would a street thug be interested in a boring suburban guy who had never bothered anyone? I thought for a moment before Kevin broke in, and said, "Stop worrying, man. These street punks were just out for a good time. They were not working for Vinny last night, and you need to put this right out of your head, and for Christ sake, don't say anything to Judy."

I took a few minutes to rehash the ball game with Kevin, and then I told him I had to get back to work. The insurance business was a nonstop paper chase, and I had taken so much time off in the recent past. I needed to be on top of my game while I was in the office. I pondered what Kevin told me and tried to put it out of my mind.

Chapter 20
David Mills

Labor Day weekend was in full swing, and Judy's sister Terry and her husband Brian had invited us, along with Judy's parents and many of the neighbors, over for their annual Labor Day barbecue. There had to be about twenty people in attendance between family and neighbors.

Brian was attending to the gas grill and cooking duties. Judy and Terry were shuttling food from the kitchen to the patio. Judy's father was bartending, which gave him an excuse to drink as many cocktails as possible without being seen. I was socializing with the neighbors that I had not seen in a long time. There were all sorts of adults and children roaming around the beautifully manicured yard. The flower beds were spectacular, reflecting how much time Terry and Brian spent on weekends working on them and keeping them perfect.

Most of the neighbors were catching up about what they had done all summer, and who could out-do who or what family had the most expensive summer vacation, cottage rental, or trip to who knows where. The second most popular subject to talk about was what grade your child was going into, what school they were attending, what teacher they had, what extracurricular activities they were doing, and of course what sports they were playing. Everyone was jockeying for position; who had the most perfect child. It was a rite of passage in Lexington, and almost as important as who fired the first shot that started the Revolutionary War.

I was walking around the yard taking it all in when Brian's neighbor Jimmy Valence said, "Hey Dave, how are you doing?" in a jovial voice. "How about those Red Sox?"

I tried to turn and pretend I did not hear him, since he was a blabber mouth and once you were stuck talking to him you would never get away. He was a huge face talker and would go on and on with runaway stories that jumped from one subject to another in a continuous succession. He talked about his family and distant friends from his earlier life like I knew them intimately. Once he ran out of news to share with you, he would segue into his job, and how he was climbing the corporate ladder and being groomed for some big job he would never get. I started looking at my watch and backing up, but he kept running off at the mouth, and moved forward with every step I took backwards.

Then I gave Judy the eye up on the deck to come and rescue me. She called off the deck for me to come in the house and help her with some nebulous task. I parted ways with mister blabbermouth, and made my way towards the house. I was so happy to be rescued, and when I got up to Judy she gave me a kiss, and handed me a snack platter to pass around the yard to family and neighbors. I meandered around the plush grass happily, and made sure I did not get near mister know it all.

I could not figure out if everyone was happy to see me or the food, or both?

As the afternoon wore on, the food and drink kept coming. There was a lot of conversation about everyone looking forward to Fall, and the change in the air from the summer humidity. It would be a welcome change , and Judy always did better with less humidity and heat. When Brian's official duties ended, he decided to start a whiffle ball game with the younger children who were starting to get into mischief. We made some makeshift bases out of flagstones, and Brian was the official pitcher. I was the resident batting instructor, and spent a lot of time showing the very young kids how to swing the bat and meet the ball as it crossed the plate.

I looked over at Judy and Terry up on the deck. They were each sipping a glass of white wine and were engrossed in conversation. I helped my two-year-old nephew hit the ball, and he started to run the bases. The other people started yelling at the little boy to run. He took up a path straight towards second base, took a hard left towards third, and made his way towards home plate with the encouragement of all the mothers in attendance. As my nephew crossed the plate, Judy's father picked him up and twirled him around, and cheered like never before. He was so proud, and everyone chimed in.

I caught Judy's eye from across the yard, and I saw her turn her head and brush a tear away from her eye. She then put her glass down and made her way inside the house. I knew what that meant, and excused myself from my coaching duties and went inside. The inside of the house was a remodeled historical structure from the Revolutionary War. It was so beautiful, and had all the modern comforts of home.

I grabbed a left-over snack off a platter, and meandered down the hallway towards the first floor bathroom. I could hear the whimper of a woman coming from the other side of the door. I listened for a few moments to make sure who it was, and then I knocked. I heard some shuffling right after I knocked, and then Judy said, "The bathroom is taken," in a congested voice. Then I heard Judy blow her nose.

I told her who it was through the door and it immediately opened, and Judy fell into my arms and started crying louder and harder. "David, I'm so sorry, but the sight of all those young children just overwhelmed me." She squeezed me even tighter, and lay her head on my shoulder. "Every time I look at those little ones, I can't get little Robert out of my head." Judy sobbed louder as I comforted her. "He could have been here having fun."

I patted her back and kept embracing her. "Judy, it's not fair," I said with as much empathy as possible. "I know little Robert would have had a great time if he was here." As I tried to make my wife feel better, another neighbor stumbled upon us, and he pretended not to see us and stepped into another room to avoid an unpleasant meeting. I spent a few more minutes trying to calm Judy down, and then we walked back to the upper deck, and watched all the activity. I knew then and there that I would have to figure some way to bring a child into our family. My mind was racing with ideas and options. I wanted to be able to give Judy what she deserved, and I knew if I did she would be a great mother.

Chapter 21
Kevin Allen

I stood on the steps of Boston Police headquarters. The sun was shining, the pigeons were flying, and the hum of traffic bounced around my head. I was hoping not to run into David Mills this morning, since he was working in one of those big insurance buildings. If he was to see me I would have a lot of explaining to do, even though I could tell a white lie and say I was there on official corporate business related to my job. I was hoping it would not come to that.

I looked down at my watch, and it read eleven o'clock. I started getting nervous since I hated to be late for an appointment. Out the corner of my eye I saw my friend Sam Kelly strutting down Berkley Street. He was a large man with medium blonde hair, wearing the latest fashions from twenty years ago. He had new black shoes that did not match his attire. We were meeting to go over all the information from Attorney Wainwright that was relevant and to compare notes. Sam had worked with me for the Boston Police many years ago, but had left to start his own private investigation firm dealing in everything from corporate crime to personal legal matters. After several years of struggling, he fell into a nice investigative gig with Mr. Wainwright, and never looked back.

Sam approached and stuck out his hand. "Well, well, well, look what the cat dragged in, Kevin Allen," he said, followed by a huge chuckle.

"I was just about to say the same thing to you." I took my sunglasses off, gave him a big smile, and we both gave each other a good bear hug, to the point a passerby started to stare. "Well I see you're fashionably late, my friend."

"Ah don't worry, Kev. Sargent McCoy will be in the same mood if we are early or late." He started to smile as we both ran up the front steps two at a time.

We entered the door and went through the metal detector. The young policeman waived us through, and we stepped up to the front desk and told the man on duty we were there to see Detective Donald McCoy. He looked us both up and down, and then picked up the phone and dialed an extension. I remembered back when Don McCoy, Sam Kelly, and myself were working together as beat cops, before we made it to detectives. We were all teamed together working the South End of Boston, and mainly handled parking tickets, robberies, bar fights, drugs, and prostitution. The mayor at the time wanted his cops to be out of the car and dealing with the public, so we got a crash course on why the city needed police, and how to handle ourselves in stressful situations.

Don McCoy grew up in the inner city, and really had a feel for the people who lived in Boston, and what made them tick. He showed Sam and I how to work the streets, and keep people safe and diffuse any bad situations. He was a master negotiator, and rarely had to take his firearm out of the holster. I told him when I left the Force that he had taught me so much more than what I learned at the Academy. He was the type of guy who could never take a compliment, but I knew inside he appreciated it.

The day cop at the counter hung up the phone and waived us through.

We made our way through the maze of desks and cubicles to Don's office. The door was closed when we reached his secretary's desk. She was on the phone, and mouthed the words, "He is expecting you. You can go right in." She then went back to her conversation and turned away from us.

I gave the big oak door with smoked glass a couple of raps, and from the other side I could hear Don say, "Nobody's home. Come back tomorrow." Sam and I looked at each other, let out a laugh, and proceeded to march into his office.

Standing behind his desk was Detective Donald McCoy, as big as life. He was the last of my graduating class that was still working at police headquarters, and had worked his way up the ladder to be head of the detectives. He looked the same as the last time that I had seen him, with black hair, some stubble, and clothes that looked out of style and unpressed. His office had an old wooden desk, with several case files on it, and behind him on the wall were many commendation plaques, promotional certificates, and pictures of famous Boston policeman and politicians. The picture window to the left of his desk had a nice view of Stuart Street, and looked back to the big blue insurance tower.

"How are you two doing?" Don let out in a bellow. "I can't

believe what the cat dragged in." The smile on his face was wide and we shook hands with each other, and then Sam and I sat in two chairs that were in front of Don's desk. We both got comfortable, and each of us had a white file folder in our lap. Don started talking about old times, and we reminisced for about twenty minutes about the gossip from headquarters, family life, and what was new around the city of Boston. You could tell as he talked he was so proud of his life, and career, and I felt it could not have happened to a nicer guy.

"Well, it seems like you two probably came here to talk about more than the price of tea in China," he said in a knowing voice. "I'm not sure if all our investigative information is related, but the only way to figure that out is to talk it out."

I jumped right into it. "Don, I would not have come here today to bother you unless I thought it was important. There seems to be too many things that keep adding up, and I feel they are somewhat related, but I want to present all that we have, and see if you feel the same way." I sat back in my chair, and then over the next hour Sam and I presented the information we had regarding Women's Hospital juvenile mortality loss statistics, suicides, car accidents, harassment, stakeouts, and coincidences. As we were talking, Sam threw a bombshell into the conversation. He told us that in the course of his investigation he found out that all of the babies who died at Women's Hospital in the past two years had Dr. Levine as the Obstetrician, and the funerals were handled by Robinson's Funeral home in Lexington and O'Brien Funeral home in Weymouth. My heart dropped. The chances of that happening were zero to none.

"That can't be true, Sam," I said. "Dr. Levine's patients come from all over the greater Boston area. How could they all be using the same two funeral homes to bury their loved ones?"

"That's not the half of it. I went down to interview Mr. O'Brien, and talked to his son by the same name, Jack Junior. He told me his father had died in a car accident six months ago on the Southeast Expressway. It was a fatality, and when I pulled the police report several witnesses reported they saw an older black sedan that cut Mr. O'Brien's car off the road, and sped away, leaving the scene."

Don McCoy reached over and took the police report from Sam and started to review it, and then said "I remember this case. The traffic that day was stopped for hours while the State Police accident unit reconstructed what happened. We put an APB on the news for a week, to find the car, but nothing ever turned up."

Sam continued. "As you can imagine, Jack O'Brien, Jr. was heartbroken, and as I questioned him he said something really strange. He mentioned his father had been very nervous the prior two months before the accident, and would get strange phone calls during the day and night, and sometimes leave in the middle of a wake for no reason and not come back for hours. He then told me that when he was settling his father's financial affairs with their family lawyer, he came across another set of books that did not match the ones he was using, and also a bank account in the Cayman Islands with several deposits made over the last two years."

An alarm bell started ringing in my head. I looked over at Sam, and back at Don McCoy, and then said, "Did you get a copy of the bank account statement and number Sam?" My heart was racing. The more we talked, the more we were opening a big can of worms.

"Yes, I did." He pulled out a piece of paper from his folder and handed it over. It was from an official bank in the Cayman Islands with branches in Bermuda, and Europe. I opened my file, and pulled out a copy of what John Robinson's daughter gave to Officer Joe Curtis of the Lexington Police, and compared it. The sheet of paper was identical, with the same format and logos. When I scanned to the top of the paper and compared both account numbers, my heart sank. The two numbers were the same except for one digit. I looked back at Sam, who was equally shocked.

I handed the two pieces of paper to Detective McCoy, who studied the evidence intently. After about five minutes of reviewing the accident investigation, the suicide investigation by the Lexington Police, and the two Cayman Island bank statements he looked up, and said, "I think it's time to call in the State Police Homicide Unit. I think we have a very sophisticated crime going on, and we need to pool all our information, and expand the investigation and use their resources to make sure nothing more falls through the cracks." Don sat back in his chair, and put his feet up on the desk, and his hands behind his head. We knew from the look on his face that this was only the beginning of a long journey. "Listen you two," he bellowed, "if Vinny Rizzo is mixed up in this, it could get pretty nasty. You two better let the professionals handle this. He has been a pain in my ass for years, but this crime seems above his pay grade, and more sophisticated than something he would normally be involved with."

We talked for about twenty more minutes and copied all the files, including what BPD had in their files, and promised Don McCoy we would tread lightly and coordinate with him if we picked up any new information. I went out to lunch with Sam at our favorite old sub shop in the South End, and then made my way back to Lexington. I was debating if I should tell David about all the new information. If half of all this was true, were David and Judy's lives in jeopardy? As I negotiated afternoon traffic on Route 2, a million thoughts ran through my head, and a sense of dread was setting in.

Chapter 22
Jonathan Coleman

My pulse began to race a little. I was not sure if this was my anxiety or too much caffeine this morning. Business in the adoption agency had been booming, and there was very little down time. I had come to the agency many years before as a favor to my parole officer. I grew up in an upper middle class family, and had attended an Ivy League college. My life as a professional person had been mapped out by my parents, except for one inconvenient incident. To help supplement my spending money in college I had started dealing drugs to my fellow students. I started by selling marijuana, but then moved on to cocaine and pills, which had a higher profit margin. After a couple of years of a nice income, I got caught up in a sting operation with my dealer, and was arrested, and kicked out of school. The district attorney tried to make a deal with me to rat out the distributor, but I was a loyal soldier, and went down with the ship and took the rap. I got five years at a medium security prison in Massachusetts, and my parents disowned me. I had a felony conviction that would change the course of my life.

After I was released from prison, the job market for a felon was nonexistent. I walked the streets of Boston knocking on doors with an unfinished college degree and no experience. I was starting to get desperate and was having trouble surviving in minimum wage jobs in a very unforgiving world. After one of my parole meetings I confided to my officer that I needed to find a better job to support myself, and asked for help and direction. Fortunately, my parole officer was a kid from the streets, and understood my plight. He had a prior affiliation with Dr. Lapierre from helping a family member looking for a child, and knew that the adoption office was looking for a smart higher level employee to run an ever growing office. The match seemed to be made in heaven, and Dr. Lapierre and I hit it off right from the first meeting. I had so many good ideas to update the office, and the good doctor was happy to have a smart employee on board who could be molded, and asked to look the other way when any unethical things were taking place.

I was well aware that Judy and David Mills were suing Dr. Levine, and that we could not have any affiliation with this couple since Dr. Levine and Dr. Lapierre were business partners, and his name was on the incorporation papers when the business was changed from the Metropolitan Adoption Agency. We could not take the chance of any conflict of interest and today's meeting with them was going to be the first and the last just in order to do a favor for Father Burke.

Chapter 23
David Mills

Judy and I stood in front of the third-floor glass door that had Lapierre Adoption Agency stenciled across it. We stood there for a few moments, holding hands before entering the lobby area. It had been many weeks and several serious conversations between Judy and I to end up in this position today. We were not sure if the adoption process was the right avenue for us to pursue in trying to start a family, but we were running out of options. Judy had been up and down over the past six months, and I was exhausted from dealing with this situation, the lawsuit, and the possible criminal investigation. I just wanted everything to tone down, and possibly to adopt a small child that we could care for as our own.

As I stood there holding Judy's hand, she held the adoption brochure that Father Burke had given her. She kept bringing it up to her face and looking at all the nice pictures of happy families with their new adopted child. They came in all shapes and sizes, and everyone looked so fulfilled and had a big smile on their faces. We wanted to be one of those pictures, but we would have to see. After some long stares from some customers sitting in the waiting room and wondering what we were doing, I tugged on Judy's hand to coax her to follow me in. I opened the door, and we passed through.

We walked through another waiting room with nice chairs and couches all over, with cloth seats, and nice oak wooden arm rests. The white walls were all covered with modern art that I could not wrap my head around. I'm sure it was expensive though. As we approached the front desk, we saw a man in his mid-thirties, with dirty blonde hair parted in the middle, horned rimmed glasses, and a nice business casual shirt and pants. He looked up from his computer as he saw us approaching.

"Hi, we are Judy and David Mills. We have a ten thirty appointment with Dr. Lapierre," I said with as much enthusiasm as possible. Judy squeezed my hand so hard, I looked back at her for a second to see if she was okay.

"Well, welcome to our clinic Mr. & Mrs. Mills," said Jonathan. "Dr. Lapierre is expecting you and looking forward to your meeting. He is good friends with Father Burke, and is so happy you have decided to come in today, and listen to what services we have to offer." Jonathan gave Judy a comforting look to make her feel more at home. "I will buzz the good doctor, and he will be right with you. Why don't you make yourselves comfortable in our waiting area, and I will make some coffee if you are interested." We walked over to an area with minimal people seated and sat down.

I was flipping pages of the latest *Sports Illustrated* magazine when an attractive young woman approached Judy and said, "The doctor is ready to see you." We both stood and followed her down a short hallway, and then took a left into a beautiful spacious office, with a view of the Mass Turnpike and the Boston skyline.

Dr. Lapierre stood up from his desk and came around to greet us. "Good morning Mr. and Mrs. Mills. I'm so glad you could come in and see me this morning. "Father Burke has told me so many good things about you." We all shook hands, and then Dr. Lapierre retreated behind his desk, and flipped open a blue file folder with a profile of us and looked it over. The good doctor kept a smile on his face, but he seemed nervous.

"Well, Mr. and Mrs. Mills, I see from your application that you have had one stillborn child, and one round of IVF?" It came out as very matter of fact, and with no compassion at all. "I assume you have tried to have a family in the conventional way?"

Judy was looking down in her lap at the brochure, and folded hands, and looked up quick as though she was slapped in the face. Dr. Lapierre's opening questions seemed too direct, and was not the sort of thing that you would want to start off with to get a conversation going to make all parties feel comfortable with the adoption process. She looked up at the doctor, then back at me, and gave me a look of dread. The feelings of her dead son were streaming back into her mind, and she was trying to suppress them and deal with the mission at hand.

I jumped in to try and lighten the mood and keep things on track. "Dr. Lapierre, we are so glad that Father Burke has referred us to you. We have heard so many good things about your agency, and feel that you have the Midas touch to help a family such as ours to adopt a nice healthy child. We have filled out your questionnaire in full, and all the pertinent information should be in there." I paused for a moment and then continued. "We are looking to adopt a newborn baby, or a one year old, but not any older. All the literature we have read says we would have the best chance to raise a healthy, happy child, the younger they are."

Judy looked over at me with a knowing smile, and gave Dr. Lapierre a nod that indicated that she agreed with everything I had just said.

"Well you two, the children we have for adoption come in all shapes and sizes. It says from your application that you would like a white American-born baby. Is that correct?"

"Yes, yes, " I said, and Judy agreed.

"I'm sure you know this will be a very expensive process for a young American-born baby," the doctor expounded. "They are in high demand, and the supply is not what we would always like."

I spoke up. " How much are we talking about Doctor? The prices were not in the brochure, and we have never done anything like this before." My stomach was starting to churn. I knew the IVF was very pricy, but I could assume this was going to be more so.

Dr.Lapierre sat forward and straight up to assume a commanding stature and said, "A white baby will cost about fifty thousand dollars, and a one year old will be about forty thousand. The timeframe on finding one will also be six months to two years. We have so many couples who come through our office, and they want the same thing you want." He paused to collect his thoughts. "After a few years, if we are not able to comply with your request, we usually refer people to another agency that specializes in Russian and Asian-born children. They cost a lot less, and are more abundant," he confided.

Judy looked like she had had a glass of cold water thrown in her face. Father Burke had made the good doctor out to be something of a miracle worker, and very compassionate, and she was finding neither. From his body language and presentation, it sounded like he did not want our business, and was doing everything in his power to turn us away.

My mind raced. I heard the figures, and timeframe, and was not comfortable with it. I was focused in on the price, and how to satisfy Judy's needs. I wanted a family I could raise with Judy, and all the hopes and joys that would go with it. But the process seemed open ended, the price was somewhat high, and the supply of young American children was not what I had envisioned. I was becoming deflated and going back to how I felt in Dr. Fulbright's office, looking up at a blank Ultrasound screen, after Judy had had the IVF procedure. It was any empty, hollow feeling, and it was getting worse. Why was finding a child so hard? There were all kinds of kids around this country who lived in poor conditions, and whose parents did not take care of them. Why hadn't God steered a few of those children to deserving families who would love and care for them? My mind raced with a million thoughts and dreams, and as I looked over at Judy, she had the same look in her eyes.

"Doctor, I was not aware that it would take so long to find an appropriate child to adopt," I said. "Father Burke said you were a miracle worker, and had helped many families who could offer these children a nice home."

Judy shot me a quick knowing glance, and looked toward

the doctor waiting for a response.

"Mr. Mills," he spoke softly. "The baby business is more complicated than it seems. There are many children in this country that grow up poor and should be in a better home, but our business is built on mothers giving up their child at delivery. Some drop their child off at a police station or hospital and disappear into the night." He sat back in his chair and looked down at the file, and then looked up and met Judy's eyes. "We are very specific on the types of children we supply for adoption and our standards are very high. We want our families to receive healthy, happy babies or young children with no abuse or psychological problems. This is our premier guarantee. That is why we are so popular, and in demand."

Judy and I looked at each other, and knew we would not make any decisions today, and would need to have many more conversations at home before we had a second meeting with the Lapierre Adoption Agency. I was trying to stay upbeat, but I knew Judy's heart had sunk to a new low and I would spend the rest of the day trying to keep her optimistic. We said our goodbyes to the doctor, and made our way out to the parking lot. I could hear the purr of mid-day traffic racing down the Mass Turnpike into the city. My mind was a million miles away dreaming of us laying on a beach, and sitting by the water's edge with our young children building sandcastles with not a care in the world. It seemed like such a happy place, and one that we could still have. I pondered the thought.

Chapter 24
Michael Lapierre

I walked briskly across the small parking lot of my office building. It had been a busy morning at the adoption clinic, with many meetings with expectant mothers and families that wanted a child. I had skipped breakfast this morning, and my stomach was gurgling with hunger. I looked down at my watch and it was high noon. That gave me about an hour to go over to my favorite diner in Watertown Center, and have the special of the day. This consisted of franks, beans and cornbread. I had never told anyone, but it was my favorite since childhood. My family came from meager beginnings, and we ate that meal on a number of occasions, especially when things got tight.

I came up beside my silver Mercedes and unlocked the door. I was just about to open it, when I heard a power window go down, and then a familiar voice bellowed from the other car. It was the voice of Vinny Rizzo and I always cringed when I heard it.

"Hey Doc. How are you doing today? Why don't you jump in? I have a few things to talk to you about," he commanded.

"Sorry Vinny. I am busy and have errands to do. I need to

get back by one o'clock for a meeting with a family."

"That wasn't a question, Doc. Get in the car. My time is a lot more valuable than yours, and we might have problems." His voice had started to rise.

I decided to give in to his suggestion, and opened the door of the late model black Cadillac and climbed into the passenger side. I made myself comfortable, and sat back and tried to control my breathing, to quell my ever-increasing anxiety. This guy was a business partner that I really did not want as a partner, a hood, and not a very nice person. I would have dropped him a long time ago, but with the interest on my betting loans, it would never be possible unless I hit the lottery. I looked over at Vinny and waited.

"Well Doc, I'm glad you could make time for me. I'm glad your monthly payments are on time, and I appreciate that. I wouldn't bother you in person, but we might have problems with the law." He took a Cuban cigar out of his console, struck a match, and lit it up. Then he took a big puff and blew it out towards the windshield.

I immediately pushed the power button for the window to go down and dissipate some of the fumes. Vinny looked at me with a death stare and said to put the window up. This conversation was confidential.

"Listen Doc," said Vinny, "it seems like our friends at the Boston PD have been alerted by some private investigators that some of the more recent deaths of our funeral home owners might not be just a coincidence. I have a guy on the inside that said they seem to think there might be a link, and have opened up an investigation with the State Police Homicide Unit."

My heart dropped when I heard Vinny's words come out of his mouth. I was never before brought into the inner workings of the whole operation, and here Vinny had spilled the beans of some very personal facts, and ones that I really did not want to hear. If Vinny went down, I did not want to get implicated in any situation where I could be dragged into a murder investigation. Months ago, Vinny had said the funeral director in Lexington had died from a bad heart, and the other man in Weymouth had died in a car accident. Was he now hinting that these two incidents were not what they seemed? Vinny prided himself in keeping his crew at arm's length, and not telling his right hand what his left hand was doing. If he was bringing me into the inner circle, he must be concerned that the law was uncovering facts that could bring them all down.

"Listen champ," Vinny went on, "we need to get a handle on who knows what about our little operation, and we should probably tone down the new baby business, and just work with our expectant mothers in Palmer until the dust settles." He paused, and then continued. "Your good friend Dr. Levine is under a microscope now with the pending malpractice suit, and he and his friends at Women's Hospital are starting to come unglued. I can't have this. This is a very important part of our operation, and one of the most lucrative." He put his head back, and took a big drag of his cigar, and then blew it up at the ceiling of the Caddy.

I gave Vinny a surprised look as two of my administrative staff that were going out to lunch walked by. I cringed that they would see me in the car, and wonder why I was associating with such a low life. I took a deep breath and held it until they got in their car. They were engrossed in conversation, and were not especially interested in Vinny's car.

"What the fuck Doc, why are you giving me that pissy look," Vinny bellowed. "I'm sorry you have to spend a little time with your underworld business partner, but this shit is serious."

"No, no, Vinny," I said in an apologetic tone. "I know those two girls who just got in the car beside you, and I thought they were going to recognize me with you." My heart sank waiting for Vinny to explode. The car beside us moved out of its space and disappeared.

"Oh, sorry man. Don't worry. With this smoked glass on the Caddy, you have nothing to worry about. It's just like looking into a mirror. Listen, you get a handle on your little friends, and tell them to chill out, and don't worry about the cops. I will worry about them. I can run interference. All they need to do is be cool, and go about their normal business. The malpractice insurance company will settle, cut a check to the Mills family, and we will be on our way again. This kind of shit always has a way of working itself out, as long as you remain cool."

My stomach was making noises, and I was famished. The cigar smoke was not helping either. I wanted to ask Vinny some questions but didn't really want to hear the answers. The less I knew, the less I could be implicated in it if the whole operation went south. I brought Vinny up to date on talking to the Mills family, and what was happening at the Palmer day care, and told him that we would step up recruitment of underage mothers from various sources. If we became more aggressive with our sources, we could continue to supply the demand, and maybe I could move away from the other operation entirely.

Vinny seemed to be satisfied, but I had a sick feeling that if the law was starting to tie a lot of loose ends together, it could jeopardize all we had worked to achieve.

I stepped out into the sunshine, peered down at my watch, and knew my lunch time was coming to an end. I walked out to the main street to a nearby sub shop. I would get a chicken salad sandwich to satisfy my hunger. I tried to push all the information I had just received to the edge of my mind, and concentrate on the meetings I had for the afternoon. A thousand thoughts raced through my mind.

Chapter 25
David Mills

It was early on Monday morning, and people were starting to arrive at work. There were little clusters of office workers all around discussing their weekend activities. It usually consisted of a weekend trip, parties, the best restaurant in the area, or a sporting event. I had been flagged into the boss's office as soon as I arrived. I wanted to catch up on work I had been missing due to my life outside the office, and all the comings and goings. I wished so much it would settle down, but with all the balls I was juggling, it would be some time before Judy, and our lives, returned to normal.

Mr. Hormsby was a great boss. He was both fair and firm, and knew the life insurance business inside and out. I had come to this big local insurance company after graduating from college, and went into an underwriting training program. I looked at it as all the college graduates did. It was a first job, and it would help me transition into the business community and give me experience to put on my resumé. After a few years of doing this I would move on and get a job in what I really wanted to do. Which, back then, I had no idea what that would be. Here

I was fifteen years later and still working in the life insurance industry, and loving it. I had made the transition from college student to office worker, and had forged a lot of good work friendships, and moved my way up the corporate ladder. It was both rewarding and interesting work, and there was so much to learn with financial and medical underwriting.

Late Friday afternoon, my boss got a phone call from a disgruntled agent from a satellite sales office in the South Boston area. He said that he had called on one of my cases and was treated in a rude manner. He said he was checking on the status of a very important client's life insurance application, and I had dismissed him as being a nuisance. Mr. Hormsby was upset and also perplexed at the same time. He knew me as both a good worker and a nice person who would never treat anybody like this. Even if the agent was being obnoxious. After our short meeting it was determined that I had left early Friday afternoon for an appointment, and was not in the office when the phone call came in.

I was charged with the task of going back to my unit and asking around to see if anyone else handled a phone call on one of my cases late on Friday. Also, I was to call the agent back with the current status of the case, and try to smooth over any hurt feelings. I sat at my desk for a few minutes drinking my coffee and collecting my thoughts, and then went around to my coworkers trying to get to the bottom of the mysterious phone call. After wasting my time for thirty minutes, and my work backing up, I was not able to find anyone who would admit to the phone call.

I started my day and worked on many complex files and

reviewed several medical record statements. I was always astounded by how many people had significant medical issues and then decided to apply for life insurance. I handled a few phone calls, worked on several of my pending files, and then built up my gumption to call the agent at the South Boston office. Mr. John Cooper was one of the bigger agents for our company and had a very high level of sales, and usually won many sales contests when we got to the end of the year. He was about fifty years old, brash and very confident, and had been with the company since he got out of college. He was also very knowledgeable in the business, and could discuss cases with any underwriter and win the day. At the end of the month he would always call, and give the unit manager a list of cases to push through so he could meet his monthly sales quotas.

I dialed the agencies phone number and let it ring. A nice young woman answered the phone, and I asked for Mr. Cooper and waited to be connected. As the extension started to ring, I hoped for voicemail to put off what I knew would be a very uncomfortable conversation. I looked out the window day dreaming of the Red Sox playoff series, and began to dream of another great finish. All of a sudden, the phone call was connected, and I heard "John Cooper, Can I help you?"

"Yes, Mr. Cooper. This is David Mills from the Home Office underwriting department," I responded with as much confidence as I could muster. "I understand you called on Friday afternoon to check on one of your cases, and was not satisfied with the response you got from us. I wanted to call you and get to the bottom of this, and see if I could help you with your questions." I sat back in my chair and waited for the blast that never came.

"Dave," he said with confusion, "I never called on Friday afternoon. I was away on the west coast last week due to my daughter had a baby. My wife and I went out to see the new arrival, and visit. Maybe my assistant called for status?"

I knew his assistant was a nice woman who was a retired schoolteacher looking for a second career. My boss was very adamant that it was a man that called.

"No, I'm sorry Mr. Cooper, my boss said it was a man who called, and introduced himself as yourself." There was a pause in the conversation, but I could hear breathing coming through the phone.

"That is very strange Dave. It was not me who called, but I can ask around to the other salesman and see if they called for me. Don't worry about a thing. I have to go, and catch up on my phone calls and paperwork. A week out of the office, and everything turns into shit," he said with an exasperated tone in his voice.

I finished up the phone call with more questions than answers and did not know how I was going to explain this to my boss. He would want to get this situation smoothed over so any bad blood would not work its way up the corporate ladder. I wasn't nervous, but I was perplexed, since I had a good reputation with the agents and never wanted to have anything tarnish my good standing.

I had just got back from a short lunch and was walking back from the men's room when I heard the tone of my extension ringing. I was about twenty feet away, and started walking faster and faster to intercept the call before it rolled over to the message unit. I closed in on my desk, almost side swiping my coworker next to me, and grabbed the phone. I introduced myself, and said my job title, and then waited for the other end of the line to come to life. There was a long pause and I did not hear any response. I knew someone was there because I could hear heavy breathing like the person had asthma, or the beginning stages of emphysema.

"Hey champ," the voice bellowed with a heavy low pitch. Then there was a pause, and the person started laughing. "My name is Mr. Cooper from the South Boston sales office." Then more laughing.

"I'm sorry, sir," I answered. "You do not sound like Mr. Cooper. I just got off the phone with Mr. Cooper a few hours ago. Who is this, and what do you want?" I was not sure what I was dealing with since I had never received a crank call in all my years in the business.

"Listen Dave, I can be your friend or I can be your worst nightmare," he barked. It was very threatening, and momentarily put me back on my heals.

"I'm sorry, sir, but if you have some business to transact I would like you to get to the point, so I can help you."

"Well, well, well, champ. I'm going to get to the point. You and your wife better drop your lawsuit with Dr. Levine. Also tell your friend Kevin Allen he better butt out of things that have nothing to do with him."

My stomach dropped when I heard his words. My mind was not on my home life and was entirely on work related issues. My brain was trying to switch gears, and I was collecting my

159

thoughts to remember where we were at on the malpractice suit, and anything that Kevin Allen had told me lately. I was at a loss, since I had not heard from Attorney Wainwright recently, and only thought depositions were progressing. But what was he talking about with reference to Kevin Allen? He had nothing to do with the case officially, and was not working on anything at the moment except his corporate security job.

"Who is this?" I shouted. I quickly looked around, and my coworkers looked over briefly probably thinking it was an unruly agent that was looking to get a case approved. "Listen, what is your name, and what do you want?"

He responded with a very thick Italian accent. "I know who you are, your wife, your friends, and where you live. If you know what's good for you, you will drop everything, and go back to your nice little suburban life." He started laughing with a very scary tone.

I was back on my heels when I heard his response. I had no idea what I was dealing with. Who was this person, and what did he want with us? Dr. Levine had messed up, but was highly ethical, and the malpractice insurance company would never resort to these tactics. I was mystified and scared at the same time. When I went back to respond to my mysterious caller, the line was dead. The call had been terminated, and I had more questions than answers. I sat there looking at a picture of Judy and both our families on my desk. The reality of the situation was starting to sink in. Money was not going to make this situation better. My family's safety was the most important thing to me, and I would have a serious conversation about the lawsuit with my friend Kevin when I got home from work.

Chapter 26
Jason Wainwright

I sat at my desk on a rainy Monday morning in Boston. It had been a busy morning preparing paperwork for trial, and depositions on multiple liability cases I was working on. It seemed like with all the rules and regulations with businesses there should not be so many things going wrong, and people being injured. My weekend had been busy touring the many colleges that my daughter had applied to, and the visits were painful since I had to accompany my ex-wife to all the visits. I had to strain to keep a positive attitude for my daughter, since the divorce was anything but cordial. The scars still ran deep, but I was determined to be an active part of my daughter's life and be the father I hoped I could be. The alimony payments would keep going for a long time, but the child support would end soon. I had agreed to pay for a college of our daughter's choice, and support her until further notice.

I looked across the desk at Dr. Michael Corcoran, my professional witness for medical malpractice suits. He was around fifty-five years of age, retired from being a board certified internist, and made extra money consulting on medical liability cases, since he had been disabled from a bad motor scooter accident in Bermuda several years ago. The money was good, and his services were in great demand. Dr. Corcoran had a great outgoing personality, and was very versed on medical matters, and had the ability to sway a jury around to his way of thinking. He was also very comfortable being challenged by defense attorneys.

Dr. Corcoran was looking down at the medical records from the Mills malpractice case which numbered about one hundred and fifty pages from the beginning of conception to the date of delivery. It contained medical notes from Dr. Levine, lab tests, ultrasound tests, and various notes on check up visits. He was pouring through all this material, trying to pick out any irregularities that Dr. Levine might have overlooked during the Mills' pregnancy and delivery. I was studying his face, watching for any reaction.

I was reviewing the depositions from Dr. Levine, the two nurses Colleen McKay and Susan Church, and several of the Boston College nursing students. The students had been traumatized by the whole ordeal. The day of the death of the Mills baby, the students had been shuffled out of the delivery room in short order once things began to unravel. They were not of much help since they were not that versed on the finer points of obstetrics, and what could go wrong. The only thing they all agreed on was that the baby was not breach, and they could not figure out why the air supply had been cut off, as the doctor indicated out loud.

I read further into the two nurses' depositions. They were both identical, and lined up with what Dr. Levine said. I could put them side by side and they looked the same, and summarized the same facts, and came to the same conclusions. The baby was healthy when he came into the hospital, and for some unknown reason the umbilical cord got tangled up, and they were not aware of it from the last ultrasound. As the baby came down the birth canal, it became clear something was wrong since the fetal heartbeat decreased rapidly. An emergency C-section was authorized, but the baby was in respiratory arrest when the doctor finally could remove the baby from the mother.

According to the depositions at that point Dr. Levine and Dr. Johnson began CPR, and worked on the baby's lungs. The process took about fifteen minutes before the child was pronounced deceased, and then the mother was sent back to the recovery room with her husband. Dr. Johnson called the hospital morgue to send someone up, and take the deceased infant down to the morgue to be processed and given last rights by the hospital chaplain, since the child was Catholic, and then make arrangements with a local funeral home.

As I scanned further through the paperwork, Dr. Corcoran looked up and said, "Jason, something looks a little strange from the end of these hospital records."

"What do you mean, Dr. Corcoran?"

He fumbled through the end of the record, and kept flipping pages looking like he had missed something. He went back and forth a few times, and then pushed his glasses up from his nose, looked straight at me and said, "There is something inconsistent with the depositions from the doctors and nurses, and the end of the file. The medical record does not mention an employee from the morgue coming up to take the body. It does not mention the name of the chaplain who gave the baby last rights, and no name of a sign off when the body was released to a funeral home." He spun the paperwork around for me to review what he had just read.

The medical notes looked straight forward. It looked as though the baby died, and then the process just stopped. This conflicted with what the people in the room said during their depositions. It was odd, but with all the confusion that day, maybe the final notes just never got into the file. I figured their priority had probably been on the family, and not on the paperwork. I pushed the notes back to Dr. Corcoran, who looked back at me.

"Listen, Jason, it is unusual that these notes don't have a final disposition of the body, but I have seen it happen before. Do you have Dr. Johnson's deposition? I want to see what he said happened after they stopped CPR on the child."

"I don't have a deposition for Dr. Johnson," I said. "He died in a scuba diving accident in the Cayman Islands six months after the date of these records."

"Well, that would have been vital information, since we don't have anyone else who was in the room that day to shed any light on what they think went wrong." The doctor frowned. "This case does not look like anything out of the ordinary, except we cannot determine why the child stopped breathing all of a sudden." He sat back in his chair, scanning the view out the window. "I would not go to court with this case. I would try and settle. There is statistical evidence that a few mothers die giving childbirth, and a few fetuses die before or during childbirth. It is very unusual, but it does happen."

We pored over the documents a second and third time to pick up any more inconsistencies. I could try and settle with the insurance company, and avoid a protracted court proceeding, but I had a feeling that there was more to this case that had not come to the surface yet. There were too many unanswered questions, and I wanted to put my best foot forward for the Mills family and try and bring them some justice for this terrible tragedy. I had worked in this business for a long time, and seen it all, but for some unknown reason this case stuck with me. It bothered me more than most.

I decided to confer with my lead investigator Sam Kelly and see if he could beat the bushes for more facts that could help the case.

Chapter 27
David Mills

I was sitting in my favorite local breakfast stop in Lexington nursing my second cup of coffee. I had been coming to this place since my big brother took me here when I was little. Monday through Friday it was filled with construction people and guys in the trades, and on the weekends it was attended by the local town folk who were looking for a good breakfast and lunch at a reasonable price. You could always get friendly service, and catch up on the latest town gossip.

I was meeting Kevin Allen here this morning, to get to the bottom of what was going on with my malpractice suit and why I had been getting threatening phone calls. The last call had unnerved me, and I did not want any of this turmoil to snowball into my home life with Judy. There seemed to be too many coincidences going on, and most were being directed at me, and my family. It was getting to the point of no return, and I had to get some straight answers from Kevin. I moved a light brown envelope around on the table, with my name and address and no return address. I wanted to make sure I did not spill my coffee on it because it was so valuable.

I looked up to flag a waitress to warm up my coffee and saw Kevin coming through the door, scanning the patrons. I raised my hand and waved him over, and stood up. He hurried over, shook my hand and apologized for being late.

"I'm so sorry Dave. The traffic getting across town was a bitch. I think with such a nice day, and no wind, the people are getting the last of their leaves and outdoor chores done before winter starts setting in." His voice reflected his exasperation.

"No problem Kevin. I had the same trouble coming from the other direction. There are many sports activities going on in town today, and the shortcut to the mall is stacked up anticipating the holidays. I'm sorry to drag you over here, but I need to talk to you about the malpractice case."

Kevin's face dropped a little anticipating the worst. He knew my heart was not in this malpractice suit, and Judy was less interested in it. I just wanted to turn the page, and continue with the adoption route. It just seemed there was too much going on, and starting a family was more important than chasing our old Obstetrician for money. I was never a lawsuit kind of guy and this process was wearing us out. The money would be good to cover some of the expenses of the adoption, but the trouble was not worth it.

Kevin heard the words coming out of my mouth and tried to cut me off at the pass.

"Listen Dave, I know this process has been hard, but attorney Wainwright has been working his ass off, and his investigator Sam Kelly has been turning over every stone in order to prove your case," he said with a sympathetic tone. "He is building a hell of a case, and this lawsuit should be a slam dunk."

"No, no, that's not what I mean, Kevin. I wanted to tell you what happened the other day at the office, and then I have something to show you." I sat back as the waitress approached. I handed Kevin a menu, and he scanned it for a minute. I already knew what I wanted, and we quickly ordered and the waitress was gone in a flash, moving on to the next party. "Yesterday at work I was called in to the boss's office, and he said an agent complained about my service. I thought it was odd since I had the prior afternoon. When I called the agent back to apologize for my poor service, he said he did not call, and was on the west coast that day." Kevin looked back at me with a pensive look and nodded to continue. "Then right after I hung up the call, I got another crank call from a man who knew about the call, and said this would continue if I did not back off the lawsuit. I tried to question him, but he hung up the phone. He also threatened my family if this did not cease. I was very upset, and this is the last thing I need to deal with."

"I can't believe these people. Who would threaten you and your family over a little malpractice suit?" Kevin sputtered. "This doesn't make sense. Why would a malpractice insurance company go out of their way to hire people to try and get you to drop the case? They have all this stuff calculated by actuaries, and just raise doctor's rates if the claims ratio exceeds the expected results."

I sat back in my chair knowing exactly what he was getting at, since I was in the insurance game and dealt with pricing actuaries all the time in meetings. They were very conservative creatures, and always looked at the law of large numbers before coming to their final assumptions.

169

"Listen Kevin, I have something here to show you." I slid four pieces of paper out of the envelope and handed them to Kevin. It consisted of an excel spreadsheet with names of doctors at Women's Hospital and all their mortality statistics. It went back the last five years and was very in depth. It also was obviously an internal document, and not meant for public consumption.

Kevin studied the document very carefully, not saying anything. I did not interrupt, and let him digest the whole thing. It was a dagger in the heart of one Dr. Joseph Levine, and confirmed my worst fears. The loss statistics for the past few years had been horrible, to the point that the hospital administration should have stepped in and taken away his privileges at that medical institution. I couldn't believe what I had seen, and as I studied Kevin's face, his jaw was dropping.

"Holy shit, Dave," he said, almost shouting. Several parties sitting around us sat up and took notice. "This is unbelievable," he said more quietly, "how did you get this document?" He handled the paper as if it was a million dollars in cash.

"I received it in the mail. It had no return address, and the postmark was from Providence, Rhode Island. It had no company logo on the envelope, and was mailed to me about three days ago. The only thing I can tell you is I got a weird phone call from the malpractice company, by a man who identified himself as the claims examiner."

"What do you mean, Dave? That does not sound right. Why would this guy call you, when you are suing his company?"

"His name was Bruce Durgan, and he seemed to be looking at the same report we have here, and even he was distraught at how bad the loss ratio was for juvenile mortality. I was also shocked that he would ever make that call, but he said his boss did not want to deal with it, and was getting pressure to fight this in court since if they settled the figure would be too large. He could not sit by and see Dr. Levine fight this and stay in practice, since the evidence shows he is clearly incompetent."

Our breakfast arrived and Kevin put the document back in the envelope, and we started eating for a while in silence. He had a pensive look on his face, and I was wondering about all the thoughts that were racing in his mind. How could Dr. Levine go on practicing, and if he really was losing it, how many more families would be affected the way Judy and I had been? What state board was watching over him, and why hadn't they reacted to this downturn in expertise?

"Listen Dave, I am going to give this to Jason Wainwright, and he is going to have a field day with it. You might as well get yourself prepared for a settlement in the millions, because if this stuff went to court it would be too damaging."

"Well, I don't want to give you my only copy, so after we are finished here, can you follow me to the library so we can photocopy it?"

"Sure Dave," he shot back. "This stuff is pure gold. I still can't believe that guy from the insurance company would ever do this. This case, and settlement, is going to take a big chunk out of their bottom line." Kevin handed me back the envelope and flagged the waitress for another refill of his coffee.

"Don't mention any of this back to Judy. She does not know about it, and I just want her to focus on the adoption process, and her job at the church. She has been through enough, and does *not* need to know all the particulars about the case," I confided.

"No problem, Dave. I will give a copy of this to Wainwright and let him run with the ball. Women's Hospital is going to shit themselves when this little document shows up in negotiations."

"I want this guy to retire after this is all over Kevin. He should not be practicing medicine under any circumstances. We don't know how many families he has affected with his malpractice, and I don't know how many hospitals he has privileges at in the Boston area. This might be just the tip of the iceberg."

Kevin and I sat for a while, catching up on the sports scene and the news of the day, and then went to copy the documents and went on our way. I had a busy day of landscaping and catching up on things around the house. Judy volunteered for a flea market at the church, and would not be home until later in the afternoon. I latched on to what Kevin had told me about the case and was hoping for a quick settlement so Judy and I could move on. How I wished things would get back to normal. Little did I know, things would never be normal for us.

Chapter 28
Judy Mills

I sat in the pew listening to Father Burke say the eight o'clock mass at Saint Joseph's Church on an early weekday morning. It had been a habit of mine since little Robert had passed away. I listened carefully to the sermon, in which the Father was telling people to be patient with their fellow man, and be accepting of the way things were. I sat there, relating everything back to David and my circumstances, and why God was testing us. We were good people, and had always been charitable to others and thought of others before ourselves.

My biological clock was ticking, and I so wanted to be a mother, and have a child to love, and raise as our own, with David. I tried to stay positive and looked up to God as a compass as to what was to come.

After Mass was over, I walked across the hallway from the church and went into the office area. I talked to my coworkers for several minutes, and then settled into my seat and looked over the tasks I needed to accomplish today.

I opened my desk drawer to get a pen and saw the adoption pamphlet from Lapierre Adoption Services. We had not heard from Dr. Lapierre in some time. I had assumed that once the paperwork was processed he would call or write for us to send an initial deposit. I was sure all this stuff was expensive, but David said he would support the process. We could find a child that we could love and raise as our own.

At the end of the day, I walked out to my car and started scanning my pocketbook for my keys and my food shopping list. When I finally found them and then looked up, I saw a big shiny black car with smoked windows parked right beside my car. I had to turn sideways to unlock the car and squeeze in. I thought it was rude that someone would do this, but then figured it might be an elderly driver who did not negotiate the parking very well.

I pulled out of the church parking lot and headed to the grocery store. I turned on the radio to listen to some music, but when I looked in the rearview mirror I noticed that the big black car was now behind me. I did a double take to make sure it was the same, and confirmed it was so. Who could this person be, and what would they want with me? I tried to regain my composure and focus on the task at hand. I would continue on to the store and stay in an area with a lot of people.

I raced around the store and tried to execute my list in record time. I had promised David a nice dinner tonight and wanted to cook it with all the fixens. As I left the store, I looked around the parking lot for the black car. Once I was satisfied I was not being followed, I unloaded my groceries, and jumped into my car.

Suddenly there was a knock on my window. I was prepared to see one of my neighbors or family members, and was startled to see a big man with a dark tan, greasy black hair combed back, wearing a medium length black leather jacket. He had on sunglasses and had a very threatening look on his face.

My heart almost leaped out of my chest. He pointed down for me to put down my window. I was now scared, and felt alone in the busy parking lot. What did this man want? I rolled down my window about an inch to see what he wanted, and then he said "Lady, your back up light is out. You better get that fixed. I almost did not see your car moving as I approached."

I looked at him with great anticipation to see his next move, and then he started to walk away with his bag of food items, and walked to the end of the parking lot. I pulled the car out and started following him. I wanted to see if he got into that big black car that was behind me at the church.

To my surprise, he got into a red sports car that did not look like anything I would have anticipated him driving. My anxiety level started to drift off, but the distant thought still lingered of that black car that left the church parking lot with me earlier.

Chapter 29
Donald McCoy

I sat across from State Police Detective Stephen Cahill, waiting for the son of Jack O'Brien, the funeral home owner who had died in a car accident a few months ago. Detective Cahill was a twenty-three-year veteran with the State Police, and was in charge of special investigations. This could encompass fraud, stolen property, drug dealing, murder, and a whole host of other crimes. He was a big man of six three, two hundred and thirty pounds, and was wearing plain clothes, so not to raise any suspicion as to their visit today. We both had identical folders, containing material relevant to our investigations into the accident, and the dead man's connection to John Robinson, and his funeral home in Lexington. The investigation into O'Brien's accident had been inconclusive. No witnesses could draw a firm conclusion if the fatality had been caused by a hit and run car or a mental error of the driver himself.

The door to the office opened, and Jack O'Brien, Jr. walked in. We stood up, exchanged handshakes and well wishes, and then all parties sat down.

"Well men, I was surprised that you wanted to meet with me again, since I thought the motor vehicle investigation was wrapped up and settled," Jack stated with a firm demeanor.

I jumped in to make everyone feel at home and not raise Mr. O'Brien's blood pressure. "There is no problem sir, we just wanted to ask you a few more questions to complete our file, and the State Police file."

"The file with the Quincy Police was closed," Jack said, "and all life insurance claims and paperwork for my father's estate have been completed. I wasn't aware that there were lingering questions."

"There is no problem, Mr. O'Brien," Stephen Cahill answered. "It is standard police work that is required when a motor vehicle fatality occurs, and other facts come to light." Cahill looked down at his file, took out a copy of the accident report, and pushed it across the desk to Mr. O'Brien.

O'Brien fumbled through the report, and then looked up to meet their eyes. "I'm not sure what I am looking for here guys, and what information do you feel is not conclusive?"

I jumped in. "Well sir, our State Police Accident Reconstruction Unit is still having a problem with the time of the accident, the lane your father was in, and there were no skid marks on the pavement before he drove off the South East Express Way. The eye witnesses could not clearly verify if a car cut him off , and according to the autopsy report, your father did not have a cardiac event or a stroke which caused him to drive off the road."

"Yes," Cahill added. "Detective McCoy and I still have a few questions." He let that hang in the air, and make it clear we would need more information.

"I'm sorry detectives, but I don't get it. Some accidents you really never know why they happen. It is just the luck of the draw, being in the wrong place at the wrong time," O'Brien said. "Unless there was foul play, I'm not sure why this investigation has to continue."

"Well, Mr. O'Brien, we have established a connection between your father and a Mr. Robinson in Lexington, as to handling the funerals of babies who died in childbirth at Women's Hospital. Also, they both had offshore bank accounts in the Cayman Islands that have consecutive bank account numbers," I finished with an air of authority in my voice.

"Well guys," Jack continued, "my father's business and estate lawyers have looked through all the paperwork, and there is nothing further that gives us any more insight as to what these bank accounts are and what they contain. I have no authority yet to access them, and the authorities at the bank have been very uncooperative with my lawyer and myself." He paused for a moment, and continued. "I told the police the first time that my father does not know a Mr. Robinson and had no association with him personally or through any funeral business association meetings." He sat back and folded his hands.

Cahill and I looked at each other, and then back at the funeral home owner. Stephen decided to take the bull by the horns and suggest a next step in the investigation that they had been mulling over for days. "Mr. O'Brien, we would like to have the State Police go over your father's car again, and see if there was any other damage we missed, or equipment failure we could detect. I think it would relieve our concerns and put this part of the investigation to rest."

The owner sat in his chair looking at the report, and then back at us, perplexed. "I would like to move forward with my business, and put this whole episode to rest. It has been a stressful period with my family, and my business, and if this is what you guys need to do, then I am open to it. How do you know my father's car is even still at the junk yard?"

I jumped in before Stephen could respond. "We already checked with the Dedham Salvage Yard, and they still have your father's car in their possession. We can send a team over there in the next few days to go over the car with a fine tooth comb, and put this case to rest."

"By all means men," said O'Brien. "The sooner we can get this thing finished the better. I would like to move on with my life and the business, and if this thing could be wrapped up after this, all the better."

We wrapped up the meeting with the owner, and made some calls to State Police Headquarters to have two accident reconstruction guys meet us at the Dedham Salvage Yard. We decided to get a late lunch and go meet the other team in the parking lot of the salvage yard.

* * *

The owner of the yard was too busy to accompany us to the exact location, but he drew us a map, and we made our way to the location. As we walked from one row of old cars to another, it seemed like they all blended in together, and were stacked in piles like cord wood. We were looking for a late model brown

Ford Crown Victoria sedan, and as we turned a corner, there it was. We were in luck. The car was all by itself and not stacked with other cars. The State Police guys could go all over the car uninhibited.

Both mechanics fanned out around the car, and then one popped the hood as best he could with the damage and started looking around with a flashlight. The other man climbed under the car and began checking the undercarriage. Steve Cahill and I began to look at the driver side of the car, and noticed a small dent, and black paint stuck on the door. That lined up with an eyewitness account that thought they saw a large, dark sedan change lanes and bump Mr. O'Brien's car before it left the road and crashed into a utility pole. A paint sample had already been submitted with the original report, but it did not lead to any concrete results.

We were going over the car in detail when the man under the car yelled, "I think we have something here guys!" We got down on our knees and pointed our flashlights toward the voice. The man squinted as the beams hit him right in the face. We shut them off at once, and this only left his flashlight on.

"What is it?" Detective Cahill asked.

The man pointed the beam of light up to the front of the undercarriage, and then with a screwdriver pointed to the brake line where it comes up to the engine. Most of the line was covered with light rust from corrosion, but as it turned up at a forty-five-degree angle, he put the end of the screw driver in a little hole.

"What is that?"

"Well, Detective McCoy, it is a drill hole that is so small the other reconstruction team had missed it due to the rust, and where it was located under the car." The man kept turning his head back and forth to avoid getting a cramp.

"So, what do you think happened here?"

He turned his head back to me. "Well Detective, with a hole this small in the brake line, the fluid would drain out over a long period of time, maybe a half an hour, if the car was being driven. If the driver was up on a highway where he was not using his brakes, he would not ever know until he needed to use them the next time. At that point there would be a problem."

The man dropped his head all the way to the ground, pulled a camera from his pocket, and began clicking off pictures of the brake line, and then slid his way out from under the car. He walked around a few minutes doing exercises to avoid getting cramps.

Cahill and I thanked the reconstruction team, who promised to write up an amended report along with pictures and their assessment, and get it to us as soon as possible. We walked back to the main office of the salvage yard and told the owner to keep the car as is, and not send it to the crusher for disposal.

We made our way back to Boston Police Headquarters to go over all the information we had. We knew there was some kind of a conspiracy going on, but there were too many questions, and not enough answers at this point. We adjourned the meeting, divided up responsibilities, and decided to turn the heat up on a few people who might be able help us.

Chapter 30
Kevin Allen

I sat in my car across from O'Neill's Tavern on West Broadway in South Boston. It was a cloudy day, and the temperature was going down. I had conferred with Detective McCoy at Boston Police Headquarters, and been brought up to speed on the funeral home investigations.

The lawsuit with David Mills and Jason Wainwright was moving along toward trial, and I was working with their private investigator to dig up as much information that could be helpful to the case. I was mystified why the hospital, Dr. Levine, and the insurance company would not just settle. It seemed like a slam dunk, and the case was uncovering a lot of unflattering information on all parties that would not help their public relations.

I was still perplexed about the Fenway Park episode, and why some of Vinny Rizzo's boys were sent to start harassing Dave for no reason. I kept wondering if one of these investigations was hitting these guys too close to home. I pondered the thought as I tuned my radio to the latest talk radio show and continued sipping my coffee.

I had come to this address, based on information given to me by Detective McCoy, to keep an eye on some of Vinny's boys and also look over their car to see if there was any damage to the right side bumper or fender. McCoy knew it was a longshot but felt better using me as an off the books private eye. So I took a few vacation days from my day job to help an old friend, and to cure my own curiosity.

I was in luck. The late model black sedan was parked right in front of the tavern, near the alley going to the back of the store. It looked dirty and unkempt, but the guys I was following were not going to win any seal of approval with anyone. These guys were mid-level in Rizzo's organization, and specialized in loansharking and extortion. They were sent usually to collect money and threaten others. Once in a while they had to rough people up to pay their debt and make sure the customer got the message loud and clear.

As I kept an eye on the front door of the tavern, people came and went. Most were guys in the trades stopping in for a quick beer, or borderline alcoholics killing some time and playing Keno. The food was good there as reputation would have it, and the drink prices were rock bottom.

As I scanned the sidewalk on both sides of the street, there were many people coming and going about their business. I saw many business people going here and there, single mothers pushing their baby carriages, and homeless people, alcoholics, and drug addicts meandering around trying to get through the day.

As I slumped my body down in my seat to avoid detection, I heard a rap on my window. I turned my head and was staring up at a very scary looking homeless person. His face was a mess, as well as his hair, and his clothes were tattered. I did not want to blow my cover, so I put my window down a few inches and passed the guy a five-dollar bill.

As soon as the vagrant left, I put the window up and checked all the locks, so I would not have a repeat performance. I laid back and rested, trying to keep my eyes on the front door of the bar, and the car, and waited for dusk to settle in.

I woke up out of a sound sleep, and became alarmed that the men and car might had left while I was asleep. I looked across the street and the car was still there. It was dark outside, and I checked my watch; it was seven o'clock. The rush hour had diminished, and not many people were around due to the dark, and the cold. It was time to get down to business.

I stepped out of my car and crossed the street. I approached the tavern entrance, and went inside an outer alcove before entering the establishment. As I peered through the window of the inside door, I could see Vinny's two guys sitting at the bar engrossed in a conversation and laughing. There was a lot of hand gestures. The bartender was standing with his back to the bar drying some beer glasses that he had washed. The boys looked comfortable and in no rush to leave, so I decided to head outside and check their car out.

I peered up and down the sidewalk for any pedestrians, and saw no one near. I pulled a small black flashlight from my pocket and scanned the passenger side of the car from the front bumper back to the rear. As I looked over the car, I could see it had been recently painted on the front panel, and the bumper had a few scratches on the side with some paint embedded in it.

I decided to take a sample of the paint on the bumper for Detective McCoy, just in case it could help him with anything related to his investigation. I knew it was a long shot, but what the hell. I pulled my red boy scout knife from my pocket, and a plastic sandwich bag from the other. I knelt with the flashlight in my mouth, and began scraping the paint from the bumper into a plastic bag.

I folded the bag over, sealed it, and stuck it in my jacket pocket. As I stood up and folded the jack knife over, I received a blow to the side of my head that drove me to the ground. The flashlight flew out of my mouth and rolled under the car. Then I felt a hand on either side of my face, and then my head was smashed into the side of the passenger door. I could hear two men yelling at me, and then conversing, but I was too groggy to understand them. I was then picked up and dragged down the sidewalk into the alley.

When they finally got to the end of the alley, the bigger man held me up in a full nelson, and the other guy began peppering me with questions. He reached into my back pocket and pulled out my wallet, and then my license.

" So, Mr. Allen," he spouted with a heavy Irish accent, "what are you doing in this part of town?"

I tried to answer but I was punched in the stomach, followed by an upper cut which knocked me back. Pain surged though my body. My ears were ringing, and then I heard the voice again.

"Who are you working for friend, and what do you want?"

I tried to answer, but was punched again.

The beating took several minutes, and it seemed to me that

the men were much more interested in beating me up, rather than getting information.

As I slumped to the ground, I heard my wallet drop beside my head, and a voice saying, "If we ever catch you trying to steal our car again, you won't be beside the dumpster, you will be in the dumpster." I could hear the voices getting more faint, and concluded they were drifting down the alley away from me. I laid there for what seemed like an hour, and then tried to stand up. I felt old and creaky. I stood in one place to get my bearings, and then felt my face. My nose was broken, and as my breathing came back to normal, I bent over to retrieve my wallet. As I stood back up I knew I had broken several ribs.

I stumbled out of the alley, and scared a few passers by who were walking briskly down the sidewalk to their car or apartment. I reached into my pocket, and the plastic baggy was also gone. My evidence went up into thin air, and there was nothing left to do except go to Boston Medical, and have my nose straightened and get my face cleaned up.

Chapter 31
Don McCoy

Stephen Cahill walked ahead of me up Mrs. Johnson's walkway to her front door stoop. As I looked up at the front of the house, I noticed it was a beautiful restored Victorian home, blue in color, and had updated windows with a beautiful three season porch on the right side. The landscaping looked mature even though winter was starting to settle in. I looked over at Detective Cahill, and then pushed the front doorbell. We both held our case files in our hands, and heard someone rumbling around in the house. Then the front door opened and a nice looking elderly woman appeared. She was in her early seventies, with a small stature, short gray hair, and glasses.

She looked us up and down for a few seconds, and then said, "You two must be Detective Cahill and Detective McCoy, I presume."

I spoke first. "Yes, Mrs. Johnson, I am Detective Donald McCoy from the Boston Police Department, and this is Detective Stephen Cahill from the State Police crime investigation unit. We just wanted a moment of your time to go over some aspects of your husband's death, and his relationship with Dr. Levine at Women's Hospital." I kept my voice formal, but tried to be disarming. I could tell she was not sure why we wanted to talk more about her husband's tragic death.

Mrs. Johnson looked back at us with a look of despair on her face. The past few months since her husband's diving accident in the Cayman Islands had been such a shock. She was still not over it yet. Cahill and I agreed before coming that we would walk on eggshells to not upset this poor woman, and would try to extract the necessary amount of information with the least inconvenience.

"Well you two, can I offer you some coffee or tea before we get started?"

We looked at each other, and responded "No, thank you."

I decided to get the conversation going and hoped she could give us some new clues. "Mrs. Johnson, I'm sorry we have to re-interview you today and dredge up the details about the death of your husband, but we have uncovered some facts that lead us to believe your husband's death might not be an accident."

The expression on her face turned from one of sorrow to one of being very perplexed. "I'm not sure what you mean officers. My husband was a peaceful man who dedicated his life to caring for sick children, and as far as I know, did not have an enemy in the world. He had been with Women's Hospital for his whole career, and loved his job so much that I was not sure he would ever retire. He was well thought of by his peers, and he was also involved with civic groups in our town." She finished and then looked down; it appeared that we had hurt her feelings.

The last thing I wanted to do was upset a grieving widow. Cahill jumped in to cut off any hard feelings. "We are not suggesting that your husband had enemies Mrs. Johnson, we just want to go over some information with you to see if you can recollect anything which might help us close the file on your husband's accident."

The woman looked back at us and indicated with a head movement that we were free to ask our questions. The information we compiled from the interview was that her husband went to the Cayman Islands scuba diving usually once a year, but had recently started going at an increasing rate. He usually rented a boat and scuba equipment on the island. From what she said her husband was an experienced diver, and loved to collect seashells off the bottom and any other interesting things he found along the way. His body was discovered on the bottom of a reef by a tour group also diving at a popular tourist destination. His boat had been sitting there anchored for hours based on eyewitness interviews. Once the body was sent to the medical examiner on the island, it was discovered his tanks had a mixture of nitrogen that was too high versus the oxygen content. The owner of the shop that rented Mr. Johnson the equipment had no idea how this could have happened, since they filled tanks and rented them to tourists all the time and this had never happened before.

It turned out that her husband, in the preceding months before his death, had become agitated and was not sleeping well. Mrs. Johnson said she found him in the kitchen at all hours of the night sitting at the kitchen table with a warm glass of milk. Afterwards, she always questioned him. He said it was nothing, or he had a hard day with a sick child at the hospital. She felt he was off since this never seemed to affect him this way in the past.

I wanted to move on to the financial business, but I was not sure how to broach the subject with her without raising suspicion that something was out of order.

"Have you ever suspected your husband was having financial difficulties?" I asked.

Cahill looked back at me, a little put off since I had just jumped in. The question had sounded abrupt, which I regretted the instant it came out of my mouth. I was so used to questioning criminals that I was programed to shock people into telling me things they did not want to divulge.

"My husband had a thriving pediatric practice, and money has never been an issue as far as I can remember. My husband always handled the money in the house, but he never indicated any financial stress to me." She sat back in her chair and folded her hands, clearly hurt.

"I did not mean to indicate you were having a problem with money Mrs. Johnson," I stressed. "This is just a standard question when we are not sure as to the cause of death."

She looked back at him, surprised, and said, "Well detective as far as I know the cause of death was asphyxiation. That is what the accident report and the death certificate indicate."

"Well, Mrs. Johnson, do you know if your husband had a bank account in the Cayman Islands, or did he just bring spending money with him when he went down there?" I figured that question was innocent enough.

"Well officers, I'm not sure." She got up from her seat and left the room without saying a word. Cahill gave me a look of disgust, thinking I had really blown this line of questioning and upset a grieving widow who was just trying to move on with her life after the loss of her husband.

Mrs. Johnson came back onto the porch with several brown paper files, and placed them on the coffee table in front of us. I looked over at Cahill, who had a look on his face that indicated we had just struck gold. I didn't say a word, and let him do all the talking.

"Mrs. Johnson," asked Cahill, "what is all this?" He looked back at me, and then back to her.

"Well officers, these are all my husband's financial records from his pediatric practice, and our personal financial records. It seems like you both feel my husband's death was not an accident, and I wanted to be as helpful as possible in case you are right." She had an air of confidence in her voice that they had not heard before.

Cahill looked down at the files, and then asked, "Mrs. Johnson, are you offering to us to review these files with your permission? Could we take them back to our office to review them, and photocopy any documents that we feel would help us with our case?" He sat forward, expecting her to say no, and only to review them in her presence.

"Yes that's fine officers. My husband had nothing to hide, and I'm sure after you review all of our financial affairs that you will agree with me. The accident report, death certificate, the life insurance settlement check, and company information are also in those files. Feel free to look at them as long as you wish."

Steve Cahill pulled out an authorization from his briefcase for Mrs. Johnson to sign, giving us permission to take the files and copy any we deemed useful. She signed the form, and we thanked her for her cooperation, and left in minutes before she changed her mind.

We raced back to the State Police barracks in Westborough which was the headquarters for the investigation unit of the State Police. While reviewing the documents we uncovered a treasure trove of information which indicated Dr. Johnson was involved with Dr. Levine and Dr. LaPierre in some sort of business venture. We also discovered an offshore bank account in the Cayman Islands, from the same bank as the two funeral home directors, and only one digit off from their bank account numbers. We handed the files over to a forensic accountant, for him to analyze more to see if there was anything else to be extracted. Only time would tell.

Chapter 32
Sam Kelly

I walked into the Middlesex Courthouse and went through security. The two officers on duty looked into my briefcase, and I took out my car keys and wallet, and they let me pass through the metal detector.

As I made my way further to the back of the building, I saw a sign saying Register of Deeds and Records. My boss, attorney Jason Wainwright, had sent me there to look for some incorporation records for Dr. Levine, to assist him in rounding out their information for the upcoming malpractice trial. My boss always liked to be armed with as much information as possible in order to help his case be a winning one.

I passed through the big mahogany doors and made my way to the receptionist desk. My favorite person was sitting behind the desk. I had it made. Mildred would give me access to any records, and let me meander here and there, due to the fact she had a long-standing crush on Jason Wainwright from years ago. In the old days he would come in and do his own research, before he hired me to do research and private investigations. They had dated a few times before the good attorney settled down with another woman. She had aged over the years, but still, looking at her closely, you could imagine that she was a beauty in her younger years. She was a lifelong county employee, and had never married.

I stepped up to the desk and gave Mildred my most hardy hello, and proceeded to shoot the breeze with what she was up too, what attorney Wainwright was doing, and the latest gossip from the political or business scene around Boston. As the conversation began to wither due to time restraints, I asked for the docket number of Dr. Levine's articles of incorporation records, and then was assigned a temporary computer password to access the details of those records. I thanked Mildred, and then walked over to the rows of computer terminals for that expressed purpose.

As the computer in front of me came to life, a big logo of Middlesex County came up in blue and white letters. I progressed through the screens, and then typed in the docket number for Dr. Levine's incorporation record. The computer paused for a few seconds while it found the correct file in the thousands of files from businesses in Massachusetts.

As I sat there thinking about all the cases I had in my queue for the next week, Dr. Levine's file came to life on the screen. The name of the company was J. Levine Obstetrical Services Inc. The address was the same street number and city as Women's Hospital, with a different suite number. I started reading down through all the information, and keyed in on when this company was incorporated, what the purpose of the business was, the amount of money involved in setting up the business, and then the officers of the company. One name caught my eye.

The name was a Michael Lapierre. I scoured the rest of the file, and found nothing interesting or out of the ordinary. I hit the print button, and wanted to do more research on Mr. Lapierre. I left his bag on the table to not lose my seat and computer, and walked to the photocopy machine and pumped in several quarters to print my pages. I always brought a roll of quarters with me, since the less you had to bother the clerks here, the better.

I returned to the main desk and asked Mildred if she could check her computer for any articles of incorporation for one Michael Lapierre. She looked up and noticed that it was me again and smiled. She typed the name into the computer. She looked at the screen intently, and then turned back to me.

"It looks like Mr. Lapierre has two businesses, one in Suffolk County and one in Hamden County. It looks like you will need to go to the register of deeds in those two counties to obtain the records."

Suffolk court would not be a problem. My boss's office was right next to the courthouse. The courthouse in Hamden County would be a two-hour ride out and a two hour ride back to Boston in traffic. I stood there for a few moments and thought about a quick-witted response which could spur some action.

"I'm sorry to hear that, Mildred," I responded with as much empathy in my voice as possible. "Attorney Wainwright needs this information for court tomorrow, and I will not be able to get to Hamden county until later in the week. It would really help his case to have this information."

Mildred sat there for a few seconds and pondered the thought, and started flipping her hair from one side to another with nervous anticipation. I saw her per pull out a piece of paper and write two passwords on it, and then slide it across her desk to me. She looked up and said, "You don't know where you got this from." Then she gave me a sly smile, and turned back and continued her paperwork.

I went back to the cubicle and sat down. I typed in the password for Suffolk county, and then put in Michael Lapierre's name, and low and behold a file flashed up on the screen. It read Metropolitan Adoption Services, with an address in Newton, Massachusetts, with the normal information contained in the file. Nothing seemed out of the ordinary, except at the end of the file there was an addendum that had another docket number, and so I typed it in. A file came up on the screen that said Lapierre Adoption Services at the same address. I paged down through the information, and when I read down through the officers, Dr. Joseph Levine was one, and Dr. Gerald Johnson. I would have to thoroughly investigate this before Attorney Wainwright went to court with the malpractice case. I printed the pages, and then sat back for a minute.

After a few minutes of looking around and people watching, I typed in the password for Hamden County, and then typed in Michael Lapierre's name and waited a few seconds. I sat glued to the computer screen with nervous anticipation. Would there be more information in the next file?

Abruptly the screen changed, and Mr. Lapierre's name popped up with a business called Palmer Day Care Services. It was located on Main Street in Palmer, Massachusetts, and the purpose of the business was day care for children, and a secondary function of a home for unwed mothers. I quickly reviewed the money invested in the startup, when it was incorporated, and then paged to the end of the file to see who the officers were. As I waited, the computer started to stall, and then went blank. My heart sank. What was happening? I pressed the Enter key a few times and waited. The time dragged on and on. My hands were sweaty with nervous anticipation. All of a sudden, the screen came back to life, and staring me right in the face were the officers of the company. It listed Michael LaPierre, Dr. Joseph Levine, and Dr. Gerald Johnson of Chestnut Hill, Massachusetts.

I printed the pages, and then sat there thinking about what type of pandora's box I had uncovered. What could these three businesses have in common, and what were the relationships of these three men? I pondered the thought, and my next move. I knew Attorney Wainwright would want me to get to the bottom of it.

Chapter 32
Kevin Allen

I looked around the spacious conference room at the Assistant District Attorney's office. The view from the tenth floor of the building was breathtaking. I could see Boston Harbor as if it was a picture hanging on the wall, with all the boats coming and going, and the airport across the water. The planes taking off and landing at the airport looked so close you could almost reach out and touch them.

As I looked around the table I saw all the usual suspects. Attorney Wainwright, and his trusted investigator Sam Kelly; Boston Police detective Don McCoy; State Police investigator Stephen Cahill, and Lexington Police Detective Joe Curtis were getting settled in. At the head of the table was Assistant District Attorney Frank Simms. He was scanning the parties in the room with a confident look on his face, waiting for everyone to get comfortable, scan their notes, and get ready to proceed with this fact-finding mission.

This meeting was the culmination of several weeks of coordination with many police agencies and legal represent-atives to try and pull information together that all the different parties had accumulated, and see if they could piece together a picture that would tell a story as to what all this information meant.

Frank Simms looked at me and said, "Why don't we all introduce ourselves, and who we represent before we get started, and then we will get on with the meeting." We did, and once that was completed Frank asked if anyone would like coffee, water, or anything else. We all declined, and he hinted we would take a break mid-morning and then we could get some beverages.

"Would you like to start Mr. Allen?" Frank asked.

I told him that I had brought Judy and David Mills to Attorney Wainwright's office months ago to pursue a malpractice suit against Women's Hospital and Dr. Joseph Levine, due to a botched childbirth. After that many strange things started happening.

After my presentation, Jason Wainwright and his private detective Sam Kelly presented the facts of their malpractice suits, the different corporations and entities they had uncovered with Dr. Levine, Dr. Lapierre, and Dr. Gerald Johnson listed in the incorporation papers. They also noted Dr. Levine's horrible mortality record with childbirths in the last few years.

Then McCoy and Cahill jumped in with a treasure trove of information about the death of Dr. Johnson in the Cayman Islands, and the new information that the scuba diving shop supervisor had left abruptly to take another job on the mainland, but no one knew his whereabouts. They also mentioned what Mrs. O'Brien and her son had said about Mr. O'Brien and his change of personality, the car accident, and his offshore bank accounts. I jumped in and mentioned how I tried to get paint chips from a car in South Boston owned by one of Vinny Rizzo's boys, and was beaten up, and the evidence stolen out of my pocket.

After all the presentations were over Frank Simms jumped right into what he wanted to say. "So gentleman, so far today I have heard a lot of interesting information, a lot of players, and a lot of speculation," he stated with a put off tone in his voice. "I have heard your concerns, and I believe something underhanded is going on, but I cannot sequester a grand jury if we cannot come up with a crime, and persons who committed the crime. It would be a waste of the taxpayers' money, and the time and effort of many state agencies. I need to hear more, and maybe you could put some pressure on some people to incriminate some of the bigger players in this so-called conspiracy." He looked around the room for consensus.

Don McCoy and Steve Cahill slammed their files shut. They looked at each other with an expression that could kill. Wainwright let out an exasperated breath, and rolled his eyes, and asked if he could continue with his court date for the lawsuit. Frank indicated he could not until the investigation was closed, which pissed him off even more. He was giving all interested parties one month to come up with more incriminating evidence or a suspect who would flip on one of the higher ups if indeed a criminal conspiracy was taking place.

The meeting was ended, and all the players went about their business. I was walking to the elevator with Don and Steve when Wainwright came up behind us and asked for a minute of our time. A lot of people were congregating at the elevator banks, so we stepped over to the right and entered a little alcove area.

Wainwright kept looking around like he was doing something wrong, and said, "I have two names you can put some pressure on." He handed Steve a piece of paper, and they all looked down at it at the same time. There were two names on it. One was Collen McKay, and the other was Susan Church. Wainwright let the names sink in for a minute, and then continued. "Those two girls are registered nurses working for Dr. Levine in the operating room. When I was doing my deposition with each one of them, they were jumping out of their skin, and had guilt written across their faces," he finished forcefully. He let the statement linger for a few seconds.

Don looked at Cahill, then back at me and then to Wainwright with a shit eating grin on his face. "So what you're saying, Attorney, do these two people have the best chance of cracking if we put some pressure on them?"

"That is exactly what I am saying," he spouted back with an air of confidence in his voice. He then turned as fast as he came, and walked towards the elevator to catch the next one that was arriving. As he walked, he turned back to all of them, and said, "You don't know where you got those names," and smiled.

Chapter 33
Bobby Callahan

I pulled down Hanover Street in the North End looking for a parking space. I was late for my usual Monday lunch meeting with Vinny Rizzo. It was an overcast day, and the sun was just starting to warm the ground. I pulled my late model Ford slowly down the street when I spotted a guy who had just moved a lawn chair marking his parking space. As the guy went back to his car to back in, I pulled forward into the space at an odd angle, and shut off the engine. As I crossed the street the guy got out of his car and started yelling. I flipped the guy off and kept walking, stepped onto the sidewalk on the other side, and entered Lorenzo's Café & Restaurant.

The girl at the reception stand looked up and saw me, and waived me through. I looked the young girl up and down, with no reaction in return. I did not break stride as I ran down the stairs two at a time. It was high noon, and Vinny liked people who were punctual, and did not think too kindly of late comers.

As I approached the table, Vinny looked up and said, "Glad you could join us today, Bobby," with a touch of sarcasm in his voice. "Why don't you take a seat and dig in before we get down to business."

Seated around the table were the representatives from Jamaica Plain, Hyde Park, Dorchester, the South End, the North End, East Boston, and Charlestown. I was representing South Boston. The guys gave a short chuckle to Vinny's comments, and then buried their faces in some nice food and drink.

Vinny had recruited me right out of high school to join his crew as a junior member, to run bets on sports and do some minor leg breaking on overdue gambling debts. I had been trouble for my parents since I could remember, and when I got home after graduation with my cap and gown, they showed me the front door and said have a nice life. Vinny took me in and treated me like a son. I worked my way up the ladder and made the boss a lot of money, and did not cause him any trouble. Little by little, his neighborhood players lost favor with Vinny and either got whacked or ended up in the joint. I was the last man standing, and ended up with the job, and excelled at it.

Vinny grabbed his spoon, and starting clinking it on the side of his water glass to get everyone's attention. The noise and conversation instantly vanished, and you could hear a pin drop.

"Okay men, let's settle down, and see how our week went."

Joey Pulumbo from East Boston went first, and was complaining that his girls on the street were unhappy about the amount of work they were doing, and the money they were being paid. This was a usual gripe with the girls, but Joey was a good-looking kid, and could schmooze the madam to make everything better with the wink of an eye and a little smooth talking.

As they went around the room the stories got wilder, and

Vinny's blood pressure was rising. Most of it was human error, and some of the players would have to get threatened with bodily harm if they didn't shape up.

I was the last person to talk, and when Vinny asked me how my week went, I gave him a good report, as usual. I told him about the incident outside the bar on West Broadway, and Vinny was unfazed until I mentioned the paint chips in the plastic bag. He looked at me as if frozen in time. My heart jumped a beat, and then Vinny said, "The meeting is over," in a commanding voice, and everyone stood to make their way to the exit. I got up from my seat, and the boss looked at me and commanded me to come sit next to him.

"Bobby, Bobby," he sputtered, "What is this about someone taking paint chips from your car? When were you going to tell me about this?"

"Sorry, Boss," I responded. "I didn't think it was important."

"Listen Bobby, things like this are always important to me. Tell me what happened, and don't leave out any details," he commanded.

Vinny listened intently, and his eyes started to dilate, and then his hand came up from underneath the table and slapped me across the face. My head jerked to the left, and as fast as it had happened, Vinny's hand dropped back beneath the table.

"Listen Bobby, do you remember what you did with that car? You had to get it fixed?" He looked straight at me, and waited for a response.

I thought back to the so called accident on the South East Expressway, and instantly knew what he was driving at. "Yes sir," I said in an embarrassed manner.

"Well, well, well. I'm glad your memory is coming back. Now you come out of a bar, and see a guy with a knife scrapping paint chips off your car, and you don't think anything of it?" Vinny sat back in his chair. "Where is the bag of paint chips now?"

I gave him a blank stare, waiting for another slap across the face, but none was forthcoming.

Vinny looked tense, but then said, "Listen, champ, I want you to tell Freddy to take your car to the body shop tomorrow, and have the mechanic go over the whole car, and make sure no residual paint is left on the car. Then I want the whole car painted a different color. Do you understand what I mean?"

I nodded my head yes, and stood up to go, and then Vinny reached up and pulled me back down into the chair.

"Bobby, you go when I say you go. I have a little job I want you to do. This baby business is starting to heat up, and everyone is getting nervous, and the cops are starting to ask questions." Vinny took a picture out of his pocket, with two girls in the picture in their thirties, and flipped it over. Their names were on the back. Vinny continued, "I need you to pay these two girls a visit, and explain the facts of life to them, if you know what I mean." A smile came across his face, and I knew exactly what he meant. I did not question his order. Freddy would have to get his drill ready for another job.

Chapter 34
Joseph Levine

I was making my way down into the bowels of Women's Hospital on my way to the employee cafeteria. It had been a long morning of consultations and deliveries in the Obstetrical unit. It had been a good morning with a lot of positive results, but my mind and body were tired. The past few weeks had been hell, with the hospital administration fielding questions about the lawsuit, and the State Police had been sniffing around asking ridiculous questions from staff and administration. No one had anything of substance to add, but the bad public relations it was causing was a big concern for the higher ups, since they had to deal with the State medical board, the police, and the newspapers. Someone had leaked an unconfirmed story to the press. That was more than likely from Attorney Wainwright, to bolster his lawsuit. It had set off a chain reaction of speculation and concern from the public, and now a lot of people were involved asking a lot of questions, and second-guessing the medical staff. I had all I could do to keep everyone at bay and try to keep my practice going.

I continued down the hallway until I saw the sign for the

employee cafeteria. I had been going there forever. The food was very good, and the prices were subsidized for the employees as a company benefit.

As I entered the lunchroom, I could see my two OB nurses, Colleen McKay and Susan Church, rapidly approaching. In the few times we were scheduled together in the last few weeks, the body language had been uncomfortable and very business-like. There was no banter and chit chat to break the tension, and I knew something must have been up, but was afraid to ask with other people in the delivery room.

I turned quickly, and put back my tray and headed for a side door. I burst into the hallway, heading in a direction I had never been before.

"Dr. Levine, Dr. Levine, we want to talk to you. Please stop."

A hand grabbed me from behind, and whipped me around. I almost fell, and then I was face to face with Colleen and Susan. They had fire in their eyes, and I knew they meant business.

"Dr. Levine!" Colleen shouted. "Why didn't you stop? We need to talk to you." She stood there panting, with her eyes blazing through me like a laser.

"Dr. Levine," Susan spoke, "we got a phone call from the State Police investigations unit, and they want us to come in and talk to them about all the bad news that has been leaking out of the hospital." Susan was panting and stumbling over her words, trying to collect her thoughts and give me some level of respect. "What are we going to do?"

"Girls, girls, calm down," I responded with as much authority as possible. "These guys are on a fishing expedition, and are only going through the motions, due to the bad press and all the chatter. The State medical board has not gotten involved except for a few basic reviews and paperwork, so there is nothing to worry about." My pulse was starting to go back to normal, and I was regaining my self-confidence.

"But Doctor," Colleen blurted out. "They said they wanted both of us to stop by their offices, and not to bring a lawyer." She was still trying to catch her breath since she was a little out of shape. "What are we going to say? I'm getting scared that they are closing in on us!"

"Listen girls," I reassured them, "this is just the State going through the motions to keep the newspapers off their backs. They have no facts, and they have no witnesses. I will talk to the hospital legal department to get this to go away. I know it's hard, but just go to the meeting and tell them exactly what you said in Attorney Wainwright's deposition, and no more or less. If they hit you with a question you are scared to answer, just say you don't recall, and give them your best innocent look."

Eventually, I calmed them down. We all walked back into the other building and went up to our floor. I was sure they felt better about everything, but in the back of my mind I too had a feeling of dread that the walls might be closing in. Tonight I would call Michael Lapierre and bring him up to date on the latest news. I was always the calm one when the waters got rough, and hopefully he would not be worried about the latest revelations.

My stomach started to ache, and I was sure it was indigestion from stress, and not lack of food.

Chapter 35
David Mills

I looked over at Judy as the Boston Common Garage elevator creaked and pulsated its way towards ground level. The parking situation over at City Hall Plaza was impossible at this time of the morning, so we decided to park in a huge garage and take a nice walk in the early March fresh air to our lawyer's office. Attorney Wainwright wanted to see us in person, and said he had some very important information about our malpractice case to discuss with us. We knew the court date was set for the middle of April, and I figured he just wanted to go over logistics and some of our testimony. It had been such a long drawn out process, Judy and I were just hoping for it to be over, no matter the outcome. It had taken all of our energy to piece the facts together from that disastrous day, and make some coherent sense of them to prove our case of malpractice. Every time we went over the facts with our attorney it just ripped off the scab on the old wound all over again. Judy was especially worn down by the process, and I wanted this to end for her sake.

The elevator doors opened, and a bright ray of sunshine hit

us in the face as it prismed through the thick glass igloo that surrounded the elevator area. As we all streamed out onto the Boston Common walkway, we noticed the crowds of people making their way further up the path. I strained my eyes to see further. I saw a large crowd forming on both sides of the path about a hundred yards from where we were headed. It looked like some sort of demonstration, but I could not get a sense of what it was all about. I looked at Judy with a questioning facial expression, and she looked back at me. I started to look for an alternative route to get to the Park Street Station area. We could head the rest of the way up Tremont Street to Attorney Wainwright's office. As I peered around, I found no logical route that would save us time or energy, so we plodded ahead.

As we drew closer to the crowded area, we could start to see the people and the signs. It looked like a pro-abortion rally and an anti-abortion rally being held at the same time on the right and left of the path. On each side a makeshift stage had been set up for each speaker with a microphone, television cameras, and stairs leading up on to both stages. A speaker was positioned on each stage bellowing out his or her message to the participants. The crowd was getting deeper and deeper as we got closer, and our pathway to the other side of the common was getting more clogged with demonstrators. Judy had a look of fright, and I was thinking twice about turning around and going back to get a taxi over Beacon Hill to the other side to avoid this mob scene.

I looked to the pro-abortion side and saw a sign about a woman's right to choose, and the speaker up on stage was talking about feminism, and that her body was her own to control. As she made her points and projected her loud voice, the crowd became more agitated.

As I looked back to my left, the anti-abortion group was calm and collected, and better dressed. I saw several signs with a cute little newborn baby on them with a big red X across the baby's body. Other signs said even the unborn have human rights. Some signs were disgusting, and I tried to block Judy from seeing them, but there were too many. Her expression was one of fright, and her face turned a shade of milky white. Up on stage was a Catholic priest telling the crowd that abortion was murder, and a mortal sin. Judy and I kept trudging up the paved path, side-stepping protestors and media people. Both crowds had been whipped up by their speakers, which consisted of political figures, clergy, doctors, and other related professionals. As each one spoke cheers rang out, and the pulse of the hysteria was growing. Then the news stations flipped on their cameras and reporters waded through the crowd to find participants representing their side. As this started to unfold people started to throw things at each other.

I clutched Judy and held her tight. We were in no man's land, right in the middle of both crowds. I held the legal file tight to my body in case I was bumped by an unruly protestor. As I was peering around, I heard Judy scream and fall into my body. I caught her from going down as her legs gave out and turned her face. My heart dropped as all I saw was what I thought was blood. After my eyes refocused, I saw that it was a tomato that had been hurled from one side to the other. Judy was sobbing and stumbling at the same time. I felt a hand on my shoulder, and was ready to turn and punch the protestor, but as I wound up I saw that it was two Boston cops. They surrounded us, and turned us back towards the elevator we had started from. As we plodded along they kept asking how we were, and one even handed me his handkerchief, so I could wipe Judy's face off. Judy was crying, and the police could not have been more apologetic.

They loaded us into the elevator and sent us on our way. I knew our journey had ended since Judy was a mess both physically and mentally. I had my arm around her, and tried to comfort her as best I could. I knew the damage had been done, and I regretted even more dragging her into this lawsuit.

* * *

I sat in my easy chair in the living room picking over my microwave TV dinner. My appetite was off, but I knew I should eat some food to settle my stomach. The day's events, and no lunch, had thrown my body into a hypoglycemic state. I had called Attorney Wainwright and told him our predicament, and that we would not be over to see him today. He indicated on the phone that the lawsuit was on hold, and there were other things going on behind the scenes that took precedence, and he was not at liberty to discuss them. I would have been peppering him with questions under normal circumstances, but my mind was weary from the day's events, and I was not thinking clearly. Based on how Judy felt about the whole thing, I was happy for a break in the case, and we would regroup at a later date.

I sat back in my chair with a spoonful of food, and droned out to the sports channel. It was showing some baseball preseason highlights, and the latest hockey and basketball standings and scores. I tried to focus on what the two men on the screen were talking about, but it was just all background noise. My mind was a thousand miles away, and I could not snap out of it. I began looking around the living room at all the pictures on the wall of my family and Judy's, and all the happy times we had together over the years. Our parents were starting to age, which made me think how important family was for love and support, especially through troubled times. As I scanned the wall, I saw a picture of Judy's sister's family with their children standing in a pumpkin patch in a Fall scene that looked like it had come out of a *Yankee* magazine. The colors were so amazing, and the children looked so happy holding their individual pumpkins, with a tractor and hayride trailer behind them. I kept looking at the smiles on the children's faces, and I could not take my eyes off them. They were so precious and happy. As I sat there for several moments, I thought I heard an animal outside in the woods. It was a crying type of sound, and I got up and looked out the back window to the perimeter of the backyard. I scanned the yard to see if there was anything moving, and tuned in my ears to the sound. All of a sudden, I turned and figured out that the sound was coming from our bedroom upstairs. Judy had been up there for hours with a migraine, and I did not want to disturb her.

As I crested the top of the stairs, the whimpering sound from Judy came into full focus. I could hear her crying, and was alarmed that maybe her headache was worse than we originally thought. I entered the room, and saw my wife curled up on the bed and facing the window on the other side. As I approached the bed, I said "Judy, are you alright?" in a low voice as to not scare her. She turned her head to the side, and forced out a "yes". I knew she was not feeling well, so I sat down of the edge of the bed and began rubbing her back to relax her. The light had dimmed in the room with the setting sun. I felt her relax for a few moments, and then her shoulders tightened.

I turned to my left and saw the portable television on the bureau with the local news being broadcast. The man and woman talking were commenting on the abortion rally on Boston Common, and summarizing the speakers, the issues, and the violence that had taken place. The screen was filled up with people who were upset, and shouting things that were so disgusting. The signs standing up for each side were alarming, and in some cases they turned my stomach. How could so many people get so worked up about any issue that seemed so straight forward.

I thought about the issues for a few seconds watching the screen, and seeing one side standing up for life, and the other group shouting a woman's right to choose. The more I thought, the more I listened, I kept harking back to how many poor children there were in the world, and the pain on their faces. How many children in our fair country grew up with not enough to eat or lived in squalor, because the parents were too poor to support them. My mind wandered from abortion to adoption, to what mothers felt who were pregnant and scared, and did not know how they were going to get through the next day. It was such a moral dilemma that even though I was a Catholic, it would be unchristian to pass judgement on anyone.

I heard Judy sobbing and snapped out of my dream state.

I looked at the TV and realized she was looking at what I was looking at, and it was upsetting her. She had seen the news, and it had brought back that awful day at the hospital, when our precious boy Robert had been taken away from us. I replayed over in my mind as he was taken from Judy's womb, and carried over to the examining table, and the look on the doctor's faces. I had thought I heard a baby cry, but they had assured me there was no sound and the baby was struggling for life.

As I looked into Judy's eyes she said in a soft hushed voice " David, why can't we have a little child to raise? Why has God turned his back on us?"

I did not know what to say. Judy's faith was stronger than mine, and I had never seen her like this. I tried to reassure her that God was always looking over us, and sometimes he presented obstacles that had to be overcome by faith. I looked at her, and knew any child would be lucky to have a mother like her, and somehow, some way, I had to make this situation right. I did not know if we should try IVF again or the adoption route, but I was not going to stand by and see Judy suffer like this. She had too much to offer as a mother, and I never wanted to see her doubt her faith again.

Chapter 36
Michael Lapierre

The brown Mercedes was rambling down the road coming into Calais, Maine. I had just shot across the Cherry Field hills from Bangor to avoid detection. I looked down at his center console and my passport was flipped open, and staring me right in the face was my picture with my name written across it with the big United States Eagle across the top.

As I looked over to the passenger seat, I saw my trusted confidant Jonathan sleeping soundly. I kept thinking about my employees at the adoption agency, and what they would do once they realized we were gone, and the business was no more. We had made a speedy get away due to the District Attorney and the law closing in. Indictments would be served today if we stuck around. I pondered the thought for a few seconds and then it was flooded out by a million other details I would have to attend to in starting a new life in Canada.

We would be crossing the border soon. I wanted to make it to Saint Johns, New Brunswick, where I had a reservation at the Marriott, and then on to Prince Edward Island the next day.

As we approached the other end of town, I saw the river

coming up that separated the United States from Canada, and then the Custom's Station came into clear view. It looked very official with a guard shack with a red and white wooden gate that went up and down as cars passed through it, and then a bigger office on the right side, with agents' cars parked behind it. There were two Canadian customs agents attending to the two cars in front of us. They had on their official wide brim Mounty uniform hats, and looked like something out of a tourist guide magazine. One agent was talking to the driver and the other was walking around the cars and poking around.

I looked over to Jonathan and gave him a nudge, and he awoke from his slumber. He stretched his arms and sat up straight. His hair was matted, and he rubbed the sleep from his eyes.

"You better get your passport out," I said in a firm voice, "and let me do all the talking."

Jonathan did not say anything, but gave a nod which indicated he understood. We had to make this crossing as smooth as possible to avoid detection from the authorities in the U.S. Our time had run out, and we needed to flee.

The two cars in front had passed through to the other side in a reasonable amount of time, and it gave me a vote of confidence that we would have the same luck. The customs agent waved us up to the guard shack where he was standing. I put the car in gear and moved up and stopped. Jonathan pulled his passport out of his pocket just as I rolled down the window.

"Please give me your two passports, and what business do you have in Canada?" he said in an official voice. I collected Jonathan's passport, and my own, and handed them to the officer. I instructed him that we were travelling around Canada on a site seeing trip that would take in many stops and many provinces. I also told him the trip would be complete in about three weeks. The officer looked at me and seemed to be thinking very hard about what I had just said. He then turned to the younger agent and handed him the two passports. The other man turned on his heels and went into the larger building.

As I sat there with the agent right by my window, I started to perspire, and my pulse increased in beats per second. The guard looked over across the car to Jonathan but did not question him in any way. He just stared at us, and then stepped back and started looking into the back seat. There was just some clothes and personal effects, nothing of any interest to the authorities. The man continued around the car very methodically and taking his time. I knew this was taking way too long for a couple of tourists out to have a nice vacation in a foreign country. The minutes were ticking away like hours.

All of a sudden the door opened to the bigger headquarters, and multiple customs agents began pouring out, and some had submachine guns. They approached the car, and circled it like a ring of steel. It looked like a scene out of World War II in Nazi Germany. The original officer came to my window and asked me to step out of the car. The officer on the other side tapped on Jonathan's window with his machine gun, and waved him out. We opened the doors and stepped out.

The officer asked for my car keys and then they proceeded to the back of the car.

"What is the meaning of this?" I spouted to the officer. The officer ignored me, then stuck the car key in the trunk and popped the lid. The other agents started pulling suitcases and other boxes of personal effects from the space. I looked at Jonathan, who was standing next to another agent on the opposite side of the car. He had a look of dread on his face.

An officer ripped back the carpet that covered the trunk, and this exposed a hidden compartment. The agent looked me in the eye, and said "Look what we have here," with a disgusted French accent.

He looked over at the officer standing behind him, and motioned for a small crowbar that the man handed to him with perfect precision. He jammed it down into a small perimeter crack and bent the instrument down. A load crack ensued and then the metal lid popped out of place and exposed the contents of the hidden compartment. Staring them in the face was three million American dollars, perfectly stacked. As I stood there frozen in place, I felt my arms and hands being bent up behind me and handcuffs being applied.

The lead customs agent said, "Mr. LaPierre, you are under arrest," in a very serious tone. "You are wanted for felony kidnapping." The other agent grabbed Jonathan and applied handcuffs to his wrists.

I felt indignant, at first. I had done a good thing by providing so much hope to so many families, but then I looked at Jonathan and I saw his head bowed in shame. I tried to block it out, but the feeling was reaching inside as well. I looked up to the sky, and dark clouds were forming overhead. As I walked to the customs office I held my head down and tried not to meet anyone's eyes, and withdrew into myself.

Chapter 37
Joseph Levine

I looked up from my desk as my trusted administrative assistant Margaret Plummer came through the door with a lunch tray from the cafeteria with my favorite meal. It contained an egg salad sandwich on white bread, potato chips, a dill pickle, and a Dr Pepper. I had had this lunch twice a week for thirty years at this institution.

"Thank you, Margaret, for getting my lunch today," I responded with a bit of apathy in my voice. As she put the tray down in front of me, I interjected, "Margaret, I have a lot of dictation to catch up with, and would like to not be disturbed the rest of the afternoon, unless it is an emergency."

She looked at me perplexed. I was always doing rounds at this time of day. As she looked back for further instructions I waved her off, and started fumbling around with my dictation machine to end the conversation.

Once the door was shut, I opened the bottom drawer of my desk and took a bottle of pills out. I put three in my mouth, and took the soda to wash them down. The midday sun was somewhat blinding me, so I stood up and walked to the window to adjust the blinds. The view of the Charles River was breathtaking. It was early spring, and the water was cold looking and had a dark blue tint to it. As I gazed across the river to the other side, I could see MIT, and the city of Cambridge in the distance. I loved Boston, and had so many good memories. I looked up and down the river for a few minutes, and then pulled the blinds closed.

The last few weeks had been a whirlwind with Hospital management, the law department, my own lawyer, rumors of a grand jury being formed by the U.S. Attorney, and possible indictments in the near future. My mind was racing, and the future was dim. So many great memories, and so many bad things that had gone on.

As I sat in my brown leather chair, I looked around my office to see all the awards I had been given, and pictures of people I had worked with. My medical degree was on an opposite wall, with other diplomas for advanced medical training. I thought back to how hard I had worked, and how far I had come. I had delivered hundreds of babies, and brought so much happiness into the world for loving parents. I stared down, opened the pill bottle, and took another three pills.

I signed into my computer, then pulled out a disc from my drawer and tucked it into the processor. After a few moments, a document came up on the screen with the names and addresses of all the families I had ruined.

I stared at the screen, and let the names wash over me. How could I have done this? The gambling had gotten out of hand. It was like a drug and a sickness with no antidote to cure it. I did not want it to be this way.

I looked back to my desk, and took a bite of the sandwich and washed it down with Dr. Pepper. It tasted good. I popped more pills and started to feel relaxed. The anxiety I had felt started to dissipate. "What good deeds, and good service I provided for all these deserving families," I told myself. "It helped them live a fulfilled life, and it was all because of me."

I signed out of the screen, pulled the disc out, and took out a pre-addressed envelope that had the name and address of U.S. Attorney Frank Simms. I shoved the disc inside with a letter I had previously written and sealed it up. My anxiety was going away, and my blood pressure was dropping.

I continued eating my lunch and took the Boston daily newspaper from my side tray and placed it in front of me. I took three more pills and washed them down. As I took a bite of my dill pickle I looked down, and on the front page was a picture of my two devoted nurses. The picture had been taken a few years ago. Right next to it was another picture of a car wreck with a caption that said that two Boston nurses had been killed in a horrific car accident at a New Hampshire ski area. I read down through the article to get the details, but I already knew what happened. It was too convenient that they would run off the road with only a couple of inches of slush on the ground. They were both experienced drivers and had travelled the roads around Massachusetts and New Hampshire their whole lives.

The guilt rushed in again. I took three more pills, and put my head back in my chair and relaxed for a while.

After several minutes, I was getting very sleepy. I finished my sandwich, and took several more pills and washed them down with the drink. I opened the same desk drawer and pulled out another computer disc. I loaded it in, and then a highlight movie of great surfing contests flashed up on the screen. This had been my favorite sport growing up, and I had pursued it as an adult. Being a doctor had enabled me to travel all over the world, and surf the greatest destinations on earth. Surfing always gave me that feeling of freedom, and it was the perfect stress relief for a stressful business. I watched the screen and focused in on the beautiful waves, and the great rides the men and women were getting. I wished I could blink myself to that place, but I knew there was other business to attend to.

My mind and body were fading away as I tried to focus on the waves and the serenity of it all. I thought back to my childhood, and my parents. My mind was fuzzy, and I looked at the bottle of pills. I read the fine print, and the precautions, but it was already too late. I drank the remainder of the pills from the bottle and washed them down with the rest of the Dr. Pepper, and gave out a loud burp. I melted back into my chair. Everything was getting blurry, and I was happy that Vinny Rizzo would not be able to harm me while he was tying up all the loose ends.

My guilt had diminished, and I was just fading away.

Chapter 38
David Mills

I looked out the window of Kevin Allen's Crown Victoria gazing at the tree buds starting to blossom on a beautiful early April day. This was a retired State Police car that Kevin had gotten a deal on when the department retired their fleet and started replacing them all with later model Fords. It gave him the look of being a cop, even though he was a retired cop and private detective.

The last few weeks had been a whirlwind of lawyers, the District Attorney, the U.S. Attorney, Boston Police, State Police, and the Massachusetts Department of Children's Affairs contacting us and bringing us up to speed on all that had taken place after the shit hit the fan. People had died, other characters had been arrested and put in jail, and still others were at large. Jason Wainwright had tried to bring us up to speed on all the legal implications and what our role would be in the future, but it was just an incredible crime and a legal nightmare for all those involved, either directly or on the periphery.

The last time Judy and I had met with Father Burke, we prayed together that God would guide us on what was the best avenue to pursue a child and start a family. He was a great man, and always gave us good advice, but not even he could have predicted what had happened. I had always been a once a week Catholic, and went along with the program to keep my family happy, since they were strict church going people. When I met Judy she took our spiritual life to a whole new level, and she truly believed in the power of prayer. The last day we met with our pastor, we came home to a ringing phone call that would truly change our lives forever.

As I looked over to Kevin he looked back and smiled, and he clearly felt a sense of accomplishment that the police and legal community had cracked the case that I was totally unaware of. He looked down to tune in the radio to the local sports station, and then guided the car off the Mass Turnpike in Palmer and took a right-hand turn. I turned around to look at Judy seated in the backseat, dressed in a beautiful blue pantsuit and matching earrings. Held tightly in her hand was a set of rosary beads that she was going through in record time. She would not stop until we met our new family member. As I looked at Judy she strained to crack a smile, and the anticipation was written all over her face. The last two and a half years had been a nightmare, and our lives had gone up and down so much. I could not fathom how we would settle back into our normal lives, but I knew we would, and our marriage would endure.

As I looked out the window, our destination came into full view. It was a nice blue ranch house with darker blue shutters, with many children's toys in the yard with a swing set, jungle gym, and a big sandbox. The yard had a chain link fence around the perimeter of the property, and what struck me the most was the yellow crime scene ribbon wrapped around the property and the house.

As we approached, I spotted a State Police car in the driveway, and another state vehicle. The sign out front said Palmer Day Care and Children's Services. We pulled into the driveway and parked the car. Two State policemen came out the door with boxes that were labeled Evidence, and marched across the front lawn to load them into their trunk. They walked by the front of our car and looked at us, but then smiled and gave a head bob, when they saw Kevin as the driver of the car. The property was deserted, and all the children's parents would have to find other daycare services, and the expectant mothers had been sent to other like homes in the area. This location's director was arrested for kidnapping and a host of other charges and was in jail with bail denied.

Kevin got out of the car and started shooting the breeze with the two State policemen, and I could only hear muffled conversation. It was just Judy and I in the car together, and I turned to see her holding on to the rosary beads, and her lips were moving with prayer. We smiled at each other, and did not say a word. As I studied her eyes, I noticed that she was transfixed, looking at the farmer's porch of the house. I turned my head back and saw a woman in her mid-thirties in a rocking chair, with a small child in her lap. She was rocking back and forth, and the little person had an angelic smile on his face, and was dressed up in blue pants, a nice plaid shirt, and sneakers. He was so far away I strained to see him, and noticed he had blonde hair of medium length. The social worker was playing patty cake, and the two of them were so happy. Our destiny was right in front of us as we opened our car doors. I grabbed Judy's hand and squeezed it tight. We stood by the car and waited.

The woman on the deck stood up, and put the little boy down and held his hand. They took two steps down and started walking slowly across the new spring lawn. As they crossed towards us, I noticed the woman talking to the little boy, and coaxing him along. As the distance closed between the social worker and us, the little boy's face and characteristics were coming into a clearer view. I looked at Judy, and then back at the two of them. I heard Judy inhale and exhale with a hint of anxiety and adulation all in one. What I was staring at took my breath away.

The genetics and common traits in my family tree were so strong. We all looked alike, with the facial features ingrained in all of us. I saw Judy look at the little boy, and then back at me, and then back to the boy again. The social worker smiled and stepped closer. I could not believe what I was looking at. The little boy looked just like me. I thought of my childhood pictures at that age, and this little boy was a perfect match. The social worker stopped, and introduced herself as Martha Warren from Children's Services, and then told the little boy that we were going to be his new parents.

Judy knelt down to meet him at eye level, and said "Hi, I'm Judy, and this is your dad, David. We have heard so much about you, and would love you to join our family." Her voice was full of joy. The little boy looked into her eyes, and I thought Judy would melt right there on the spot. Ms. Warren coaxed Robert to hug Judy, and he did so for a few seconds, and then retreated back beside his trusted partner.

I stuck out my hand and tried to shake my son's hand, but

he was glued to Ms. Warren. I was so nervous about how this whole episode would unfold, and as I looked down at my son, all I could think of was that poor family in Canton, Ohio, who had adopted my son and who had raised him for the past two years. That poor couple had been so thankful that they had been blessed with a beautiful baby boy, and put in the time and sleepless nights raising Robert as their own. I could not have imagined what they felt when the social workers in Ohio had knocked on their door, and told them that their little bundle of joy had been stolen from another family, and would have to go back to the rightful parents. The heartbreak this had caused to our family, and countless other families caught up in this evil deed, was beyond comprehension.

As someone who was always planning, and making sure things went smoothly, I went over in my mind how we could incorporate that other family in Robert's life. I wondered if social services and all the psychologists would think it was a good idea. I pondered the thought for a few moments, until Ms. Warren asked Judy and I if we would like to go to lunch at Friendly's restaurant, and visit with Robert further. We both gave a hardy "Yes," and she got into the backseat of our car with our son, and Judy slipped in on the other side. Then Kevin and I got in, and I looked in the back seat. Our little boy was looking from Judy, and then back to the social worker to get a sense of what was taking place.

This day was one of many visits, in order to make the transition for our beautiful little boy as smooth as possible. I thought ahead to the family summer barbecue's that we would have, and this year I would be playing catch with my dear little boy.

Chapter 39
Vinny Rizzo

I pulled down Hanover Street in Boston looking for a parking space across the street from Lorenzo's Café & Restaurant. The traffic was heavy in the area for noon time on a Monday, and I was in no mood to wait for a space to open up. The last few days had been a pain in the ass, and I was sick of doing damage control. I double parked my black Lincoln, and stepped out and crossed to the other side.

As I entered the door of the restaurant, I saw Angela standing behind the hostess stand looking down at her reservation list.

"Good afternoon Mr. Rizzo," she said with a cute little Italian accent. She had medium brown hair, blue eyes, and was wearing a black little cocktail dress with just enough cleavage showing to keep people interested.

"Honey can you have the valet park my car across the street, and keep it safe until I come back upstairs later?"

"But, Mr. Rizzo, the valet does not come on until two o'clock sir." She looked back at me with a perplexed look.

I flipped her the keys, which she caught, and yelled back at her to figure it out as I was walking towards the back stairs. As

I descended, I saw a waiter coming back up with some dirty dishes on a big brown tray. When he saw me he froze, and then stopped. I told him to get my veal parm sandwich with extra red sauce and a glass of Merlo wine, and make it fast. The waiter started doing double time up the stairs and disappeared.

I turned the corner and entered the lower dining room. I saw the boys all seated in the corner at their usual table, filling their faces with pasta and telling their war stories from the weekend. As I approached the men, they all turned to greet me and offer some rolls and butter.

Bobby Callahan from Southey stood, and gave me a knowing look, patted my back, and sat back down.

"Hey boss. Is everything okay?"

I looked back at him ready to let go, but Bobby was saved by the waiter bringing over my meal and drink. Saved by the bell. Bobby was a trusted advisor, but some of his screw ups had caused a domino effect by the law that had caused this fiasco. As I looked back at him, Bobby had a bead of perspiration running down his forehead. He knew he was in trouble.

I had been meticulous to tie up any loose ends with regard to our little business, but there had been one wild card I had not counted on. Dr. Michael Lapierre had been captured by customs and returned to the federal lock up at Fort Devens, awaiting trial for kidnapping and a host of other charges. He would do five to ten years in federal prison if convicted. I got word to Lapierre and his assistant that it could be hard time or easy time, depending on if they kept their mouths shut, and did their stretch like men. I knew they were soft, and the U.S. Attorneys could play one person off against the other with the reward of a lighter sentence. I could not take that chance. They might have to have an accident in their cell, the shower, or the laundry room. Maybe a lover's quarrel, with one person killing the other, and the survivor committing suicide from the guilt. There were so many ways I could plan it, and I had the manpower at my fingertips to make it happen. I thought of the possibilities, and it made me hungry to eat.

When I looked up, Bobby was looking back at me with that look of apprehension pasted across his face. He was ready to speak, but I waived him off.

I looked down the table at the boys, and they were exchanging more war stories and complaining about their little petty inconveniences running their territory, but they had it pretty good. They were all making good money, and I left them alone as long as the bottom line looked good at the end of the month, and the big boys in Providence were happy.

I started tapping my fork on my water glass to get their attention. They all stopped in their tracks, and looked back at me. "Boys, we are out of the baby business now," I said, and started to laugh as they looked back at me with astonishment. I caught Bobby's expression out the corner of my eye, since he was the only one who knew all the details of the business and players. He turned white as a sheet as I continued to laugh. The boys started to join in on the laughter, and I sat back very pleased with myself.

Today I was going to skip my cannoli at Mike's Bakery, and have the Tira Misu right here. I snapped my fingers, and a waiter appeared from nowhere and stood by my side. I looked down the table and said, "Today boys, we are taking the afternoon off! Give the good waiter your drink orders, and we will talk over some new businesses we can explore. I am open to all suggestions." There was silence for a minute, and then they came to life.

Made in the USA
Middletown, DE
01 July 2021

43393882R00144